AN E[

AN EMPTY ROOM

Mu Xin

Translated from the Chinese by Toming Jun Liu

A NEW DIRECTIONS BOOK

The Publisher would like to thank Joanne Wang for her assistance in arrang-ing this publcation.

Manufactured in the United States of America
New Directions Books are printed on acid-free paper.
First published as a New Directions Paperbook (NDP1190) in 2011
Published simultaneously in Canada by Penguin Books Canada Limited

Library of Congress Cataloging-in-Publication Data

Mu, Xin, 1927–
[Short stories. English. Selections]
An empty room / Mu Xin; translated from the Chinese by Toming Jun
Liu.p. cm.
Includes bibliographical references.
ISBN 978-0-8112-1922-8 (paperbook: alk. paper)
I. Liu, Toming Jun. II. Title.
PL2886.U155E67 2011
895.1'45—dc22

2010052844

10 9 8 7 6 5 4 3 2 1

New Directions Books are published for James Laughlin
by New Directions Publishing Corporation
80 Eighth Avenue, New York, NY 10011

Contents

AN EMPTY ROOM

The Moment Childhood Vanished

IF A CHILD KNOWS what he should know and does not know what he should not, his childhood will be very happy. But when I was a child, I did not know what I should know, and I knew what I should not, hence all kinds of bewilderments continue to follow me today.

Before I was ten years old, I already knew the nuanced differences between the seven types of Buddhist temples: *si, miao, yuan, chan, guan, gong,* and *an.* That year I followed my mother and the whole retinue of my paternal and maternal aunts to Mount Mo-An for a Buddhist service. I didn't complain when we passed a temple at the foot of the mountain or when we reached another one halfway up. But when we neared the Shizi Mian An (Sleeping Lion Nunnery) close to the peak, I asked, "Is this the place?"

"That's right, we're here," said a porter who was carrying our luggage on a shoulder pole.

I turned to my mother. "So nuns will perform the rites for us?"

"Oh no," she said, "the leading monk here is a great master. Believe it or not, he's in charge of eighty-two temples around here."

I was even more puzzled. "Then, how can he live in a nunnery? The Sleeping Lion *An*?"

She was silent, then said softly, "Well, perhaps ... perhaps they recently moved here from somewhere else."

The temple gate was plain, but once we stepped inside the grandeur expanded: after the First Mountain Pass was the Second Mountain Pass; then there was the Palace of Great Majesty, the dining hall, meditation rooms, and the guest house. Indeed it was a magnificent temple in the ancient style! With so much to explore, I soon forgot the mystery of the temple's name.

My family never failed to honor the Buddha. It was for the purpose of worshipping our ancestors and burning *shu-tou* that my mother had decided to make this trip. As far as I could explain then, *shu-tou* was the written penance sent to the dead ancestors "by water route and by land route," the entire rite involving an elaborate performance. Or, as I understood it, a kind of bank check with a high monetary value acceptable in the other world, an otherworldly currency for penance. People in the world of Yang supposedly paid for the benefit of the people in the world of Yin. Many monks were involved in this extravagantly observed rite of complicated procedures as if it were a grand drama acted out in sequential segments with monks reciting the scriptures and kowtowing on the ground. In the splendor sustained by bright candles, endlessly burning incense, and incessant Buddhist music and chants, the service continued for seven times seven days and nights in order for the prayers to be completed in a formal fashion.

For a child, it was a curious spectacle to observe at first. But after seven days I grew weary. There was only so much to see on the mountain, and I only had to look at the Buddhist vegetarian meals to feel repulsed. I even got tired of teasing a crazy monk who was locked up in a cave behind the temple. So I sighed deeply, thinking how very difficult it was to release your dead ancestors.

I pestered my mother about going home every day until she replied, "Soon, soon. We'll go home the day after we receive *shu-tou*."

That day was finally about to arrive. I was giddy at the thought of eating regular food, kicking balls, flying kites. At the same time I worried about the instructions I had received from a hunchbacked monk. He had told me that I would kneel in the Palace tomorrow, carrying a wooden plate. He said that my hands should be extraordinarily clean and I should quietly hold the plate while waiting for the head monk to finish his *shu-tou* chant. Out of frustration I asked, "How long do I have to kneel?"

"About as long as it takes for someone to smoke a cigarette."

"What brand of cigarette?"

"Something like Golden Mouse or Beauty."

I felt better, relieved that it wouldn't take as long as the burning of an incense stick at the altar. I even laughed, imagining the hunchbacked monk hiding in a room and smoking a Golden Mouse or Beauty.

The receiving of *shu-tou* came and went. It didn't seem to take as long as smoking a cigarette, but I itched all over while I kneeled, holding the redwood plate while monks' robes and temple flags surrounded me. I felt it a great injustice that I should be suffering for ancestors whom I had never known. Still, the recitation of a monk standing to my right piqued my interest: "... aai ... the twenty four altitudes ... aai ... in the Clear Breeze Village of the ... aai Phoenix Tree and Mulberry County in the ... aai Luck River Province in the Capital ... aai ... of the King of the Under ... ai-hi-yi-ai ... world, ai-hi ..."

I was amused. So on the large folded yellow paper called *shu-tou* was written an address? But what could he mean by the twenty-four altitudes? Was it where *shu-tou* was sent to or sent from? Was there really an underworld? Was the underworld also measured by altitudes? As I considered these strange thoughts it was over before I knew it. I felt relieved to stand and straighten my back. As soon as I received *shu-tou* in a large envelope with a large seal on it, I rushed over to my mother.

"There is an address on *shu-tou*. It's the twenty-four altitudes in the Clear Breeze Village of the Phoenix Tree and Mulberry County in the Luck River Province. And it's addressed to the King of the Underworld," I told her with pride.

My aunts stood around my mother, not letting their opportunity to tease me slip by.

"Aha! A ten-year-old can understand a monk reading scripture. Who knows what lies in store for him in the future!"

"At least he'll be the favored disciple of a great scholar."

"Well, it seems he'll enter the world of Dao and be in charge of eighty-two temples." ·

My mother said with a smile, "He should at least know the difference between a village, a county, and a province. Otherwise how can he find his way home?"

I had not meant to show off and felt their teasing was unjust. After all, I knew not only the difference between a village, county, and province—I could also name seven different types of temples.

It was time to go home!

Porters carried our luggage on their backs or with shoulder poles. My female relatives were dressed in bright red and green and draped with lustrous jewelry. I followed everyone out of the gate. Taking a last glance back, I once again saw the lintel inscribed with those words: Sleeping Lion *An*. How could monks live in this place meant for nuns? Such a temple shouldn't be so big. And why didn't my family ask even a single question?

Our family teacher was an erudite scholar who had passed the imperial exam of the Manchu Dynasty with high honors. I was a piece of stone too hard to be carved into any desired shape. As he taught me, I would nod just to make the days go by. It wasn't that I couldn't memorize books or write poetic couplets. It was that I always wanted to read books that were classified as inferior. In those years, especially in my family, "forbidden books" covered such a wide range of writings that even Tang and Song poems were excluded—they were simply "not for someone your age." Precisely for that reason, I particularly enjoyed the sound and sense of two lines of Li Bai from a collection of annotated poetry, which read: "When rain stops the sky clears / Where clouds open colors merge." One day I was staring at a pale pottery vase on my teacher's desk and somehow murmured these two lines. My teacher heard and scolded me: "Where did you learn that? Remember, sentimental poems weaken your will!" Frustrated, I suddenly felt that in his dark study the rain would never stop and the sky would never clear. I dipped my middle finger in water and wrote the word "escape," though I had no strategy as to how to accomplish this. All I could do was watch the character dry up. A sour vindication filled my heart.

More than anything else I dreaded writing essays. Topics for assignments were so dry: "On Great Courage and Small Courage," or "Su Qing Tries to Persuade King Hui of the Qing on the Need for an Alliance but the King Does Not Accept: An Essay in Assessment." I know now that the idea was to deform the mind of a child as foot-binding deformed girls' feet. I had to improvise without any confidence. After a while, I would count words. If I had about a hundred words, I would feel relieved. With about two hundred words, I would feel like Li Bai's "boat sailing light, leaving behind a thousand mountains." My essays would be handed back to me all marked in red, like "a pink face mirroring a peach blossom." I would feel embarrassed, and then vengeful. The teacher's heavy editing of my essays made it seem that he was writing about the topics he had assigned himself. In case my mother asked to see these essays, I always made clean copies, leaving out the teacher's negative comments. After reading one, she would smile and say something like, "Well, you *are* capable of making something out of nonsense, although I must say it still lacks depth." I was secretly amused that my teacher was really the one whom my mother alluded to unknowingly as "capable of making something out of nonsense" and who lacked depth.

A boat full of people were waiting in excited anticipation to leave when I suddenly realized I had left my special bowl in the temple.

At home each of us had our own cup-and-bowl set. If someone accidentally took another's during tea or a meal, we would wait until the mistake was rectified. I was even given my own tea cup and rice bowl during our stay in the mountains. My tea cup was designed with one of the twelve zodiac symbols corresponding to the year of my birth. I didn't particularly care for the cup. But my rice bowl was a different story. As I didn't like Buddhist meals, the elderly master gave me a small bowl fired in a famous kiln as a gift. The bowl had a delicate cobalt-blue glaze. Any food served in it somehow became more appetizing.

"The master is a master after all," my mother said. "He knows the temperament of this little monkey."

I recited in reply, "When rain stops the sky clears / Where clouds open colors merge."

"That's right," she said. "This bowl is part of a long tradition of ceramic making. Look at its color. Only a master monk can afford such an extravagant gift. Make sure you don't drop it."

After each meal I would wash it in a brook and carefully put it away. The night before we left, I had wrapped it in soft cotton paper and placed it next to my pillow. But I woke up dazed the next morning as everyone hurried to prepare for departure. Somehow I forgot to pack the bowl. It would have been better if I had completely forgotten about it. Now that I did remember, the boat was about to leave shore.

"The bowl!" I said.

"What is it?" My mother didn't know what I was talking about.

"That bowl, that special bowl, the gift."

"Where did you put it?"

"Next to my pillow."

My mother knew I could never forget about a lost object that meant so much to me. The only way to ease my mind was to possess it again.

"We can buy another one when we get home."

"No, we can't. It wouldn't be the same one." I was certain that the bowl was unique.

"What then? Must someone go back and get it?" She implied that I should forget about it since it was impossible that the boat should wait for one person to climb to the temple and back.

I walked across the landing plank, sat on the stump to which the boat was tied, and lowered my head to stare at the river.

People in the boat were stunned and started whispering to each other. No one came ashore to talk to me. They waited for my mother to force me aboard. She did nothing of the kind, and instead whispered to a muscular young boatman who picked up his padded jacket, flew across the landing plank, and ran up the mountain path.

Mountain dwellers call azaleas "red reflections of the mountains." Azaleas—mostly red ones, some white—were in full bloom. I wandered to a bush, picked a flower, and sucked it. A honey-like taste stung my tongue. In this way I waited.

The whisperings in the boat faded. Each found something to do—some played chess or cards, others ate sunflower seeds. A few opened the fruit boxes that the monks had given them and beckoned me to eat with them on board. I waved a "No thanks." There were plenty of interesting things along the shore: pebbles of myriad hues, green snail shells, transparent gray shrimp shells.... I felt a pang of regret. I didn't think it would take so long.

Mountain partridges cooed and cooed in the distance. It had rained last night.

"I'm coming…! Coming…!" rose the voice of the young boatman, although we couldn't see him.

He emerged from a small path and slowed to a stride. As he neared, I saw him empty-handed and felt defeated—the bowl was lost! Perhaps he couldn't find it or it had broken.

With a broad smile he slipped one hand inside his padded jacket that was tied with a belt and took out the bowl. The cotton paper was torn and soaked with sweat but his face was free of any perspiration. I received the bowl with both of my hands, thanked him, and walked across the plank, holding it carefully.

The boat rocked slightly until there was a gradual, rhythmic evenness of rowing. The river unfolded like a huge expanse of silk. The pace of the boat breaking the waves and the occasional words exchanged between the boatmen at the oars created a rare tranquility. I didn't feel like going into the cabin and sat alone at the bow. It had indeed rained heavily last night. I remembered hearing thunder. Mountains, now refreshingly green in the distance, blurred in the water reflections. A mild breeze caressed my face. Where was my mother?

Slowly the river became even broader and the mountains flat. I thought I should wash the bowl.

With so many people on board, the waterline was quite high. I barely had to bend my arm to touch the river. So I filled the bowl with water and poured it skyward. In the sunlight, drops of water looked like pearls. I stood up and tried to throw the water a bit farther away when my fingers slipped and the bowl dropped.

In the swirling river, the bowl, face up, was a lotus leaf separated from its stem, floating up and down, quickly disappearing toward the stern, further and further away....

I watched something vanish, as if I was in a dream from which I couldn't wake.

What could I say to my mother? And to the boatman?

She emerged from the cabin, carrying a saucer with dim sum.

I told her what happened.

"Someone will find it. Even if it sinks, someone in the future will recover it as long as it doesn't break.... Eat something. No need to think about it. When you are done with your snack, come inside for some hot tea.... Such things won't be rare occurrences in the future."

She spoke the last sentence very softly. What could she mean?

Looking back, I find my mother's words an ominous prophecy. Such things are indeed no rare occurrences in my life. Many things and people, far more precious than that bowl, have been lost. Some broken.

At that moment, with the floating bowl, only my childhood vanished.

Xia Mingzhu: A Bright Pearl

WHEN MY FATHER was in his prime, a wealthy married man taking a mistress was "legitimate" in the eyes of the public. Besides, our ancestral home was in a remote and ancient village, and my father's business was in a faraway, bustling metropolis. While my mother, my sister, and I guarded the ancestral home, my father was alone in the city, dealing with his business competitors and partners. It thus seemed reasonable that he should have a woman there who could help him with domestic and social matters. Nevertheless, my mother, knowing that Miss Xia and my father had been living together for many years, never asked him about her. If my father had boasted of it as a romantic affair, my mother would most likely not have tolerated it.

I remember our winter vacations—snow in the ancient village, the opera singing during temple festivals—everything was joyful while we spent the New Year with Mother. During our summer vacations, my sister and I would travel by boat and train to the city. Father would let us stay in the extravagant hotel he owned and managed. My sister was a smart girl, and brave, too. She would always explore the vicinity of the hotel to find open areas for us to play, expanding our territory. Everyone in the hotel, from upper management to the staff, took care of us. Everything we asked for, though we hardly asked, was provided. Father seemed to think that nothing could go wrong. He barely had time for us anyway. It was Miss Xia who would come in her car to see us and take us to her villa for dinner. She had all kinds of questions for us, and if our conversation went well, she would ask us to call her "Second Mother." Sister and I would just smile and look at her. It wasn't that our mother had told us not to call her that—we just felt uncomfortable. Everything about her was enchanting: her European-style beauty, her good manners, her amiable personality, her hospitality. But there was only one mother for us and we couldn't accommodate a second one. Plus, she didn't look anything like our mother. She looked more like, well, a flower. Sister and I would sometimes make faces behind her back, and call her "a social flower," knowing it wasn't very nice of us to say that. Sister told me that Miss Xia was a top graduate of Zhejiang-Jiangsu (Z-J) Academy of Physical Sciences. "Top graduate" I understood. Apparently she was one of three with the highest GPA. But I had only heard about a certain Z-J governor by word of mouth, never a Z-J Academy of Physical Sciences. Sister told me that in the Academy, which was run by both Zhejiang and

Jiangsu provinces, Miss Xia was also a star swimmer and a star tennis player. Suddenly my esteem of Miss Xia ballooned. But this esteem quickly deflated when I learned of a different title she possessed. "Do you remember that huge beauty salon across the street?" Sister once said. "Well, Miss Xia is the lady boss of the White Rose Beauty Salon." I hated all lady bosses. So every time I saw her, I tried to secretly tell which of her gestures and smiles were those of a lady boss and which of a star athlete, until I got confused and tormented by my lack of insight. Why care? Sister said. I just eat the yummy roast duck liver she brings and wear the skirts she buys; it's dad's money anyway. I, too, ate the duck liver; I also wore strap pants and leather boots—all purchased with father's money. (But it was Miss Xia who took us to the store, made selections for us, and had our clothes custom made. If we had gone on our own, the store owner wouldn't have been so patient in letting us try them on so many times. He even sent our new purchases to the hotel.) As soon as we stepped into the store, Miss Xia would say, "You like this kind of leather boot, don't you?" It was amazing. I felt pleased and would ask her, "How did you know?" "You look really handsome in them, like a military officer." I was won over as she knew my thoughts. She also knew Sister's thoughts. Miss Xia envisioned her as a young dancer, and had many dancing costumes of light gauze made for her, each outfit arriving one after another like a magician's trick. I almost complained that I couldn't be a girl. Since soft dancing steps weren't my style, I clicked my boots to make loud sounds. If we were walking on the road, I certainly attracted more attention than Sister.

As our first summer vacation came to an end, Father bought us a lot of stationery, toys, candies, and cookies, as well as a box of gifts for Mother. "I'm sorry that I haven't been able to keep you company," he said. "Well, did you have a good time anyway?"

"Not bad," I replied.

"What do you mean, 'not bad'?"

"I mean it was OK."

"You are trying to avoid saying 'good,' aren't you?"

"It was quite good," I said.

"It was very good," Sister joined in. "We had a wonderful time."

Father lit a cigar and sat down. "If your mother asks the same question, you should say 'Quite good,' right?"

"We will," Sister replied. I nodded in agreement.

Father pulled me close to his chest, kissed me and whispered, "You're angry with me. That is why I like you."

During the journey home by train and boat, we talked about what we should say and not say in case Mother asked, as she certainly would. The horse race and dog race, skating, Chaplin, Uncle Hai Jing—these things we could report. Crystal lights in the villa, silver table tops, Miss Xia singing and playing piano, diamond necklace—no report. Persian carpets, clumsy clocks made in England, a marble child peeing—no report either. What about the beauty salon? Mother would stay in the hotel if she visited, and would also go to the salon, but wasn't likely to ask, "Who is your lady boss?" I agreed with Sister. We were two children who didn't understand much about values or politics, but we followed our instincts: we tried to stay loyal to Mother without betraying Father.

That evening when we came home, Mother opened the gift box. Both Sister and I were surprised to see how much the box could hold, and were also happy to see Mother try on the clothes. A thought flashed across my mind: It was Miss Xia who had chosen everything! All the cosmetics were ample supply for a makeup artist. There was also a bottle of skin-clarifying cream, so I asked, "Ma, do you have freckles?"

Mother showed me her hand and said, "Look at that. Strange I should have freckles on the back of my hand. I didn't even notice them until recently."

As children, we simply believed that every year there would be a summer vacation; every year Father would welcome us to his hotel; every year Mother would wait for our return; everything would be like the oval red-oak table in the family room, lasting forever and ever. We never thought that lightning and thunder could tear through a clear sky. But it did: Father suddenly died, one year before the outbreak of the Pacific War. Then the family began to decline. Later, as we fled during the war, Mother often mumbled, "It's good he left before this. He doesn't have to suffer like a refugee."

Soon after Father's death, Miss Xia returned to our ancient village, which was also her hometown. Her parents had died a long time ago. Her three brothers had neither property nor occupation but were dressed extravagantly like country gentleman. The locals were baffled by this and guessed they were involved in some kind of criminal activity. Miss Xia's given name was Mingzhu, which means "bright pearl," but somehow her nickname was "night pearl." Her homecoming was big news—the rumor spread that the night pearl was shattered and could shine no more.

As if Father's death wasn't bad enough, Miss Xia's bad luck deepened when she offended a very important lady boss of a foreign company. She couldn't take it anymore and came home defeated. That she even moved her furniture and piano home indicated that she would be staying a long time. Miss Xia was a delicate beauty who belonged to the bustling world and seemed out of place in an old village. She had long been damned by various rumors spread by those local "respectable elements" who said that she had brought shame to the village and had ruined its reputation. People said that Xia Mingzhu avoided seeing anyone and lived like a woman with her face behind a veil. When we heard this, my mother said in a flat tone, "She deserves it."

Mother wouldn't even consider that Xia Mingzhu returned to her hometown as a result of a life-changing epiphany; instead, she thought Miss Xia's misfortune and her loss of dignity were her own fault.

Several times Miss Xia sent someone over to plead with Mother that she be accepted as a member of our family.

She said that she had given birth to a daughter with my father and at the very least this child should take our family name. Mother offered some financial help but refused the other two requests unequivocally. Once, Miss Xia's intermediary said something that infuriated Mother. Mother's reply used words which were too cruel: "If she has the nerve to cross our doorstep, her front leg will be smashed if her front leg crosses first, and her hind leg will be broken next if it crosses after."

I felt a chill hearing those words. Not only was Mother being merciless, but she compared Miss Xia to something not human.

When the embarrassed intermediary left, Mother explained to me and Sister, "I can tell that you feel pity for her in your hearts, and you find my words vulgar. You are still too young to understand the consequences if she comes to us with that child. She is not young anymore so she might be a good woman now who will not shame us. And it's nice that you have a little sister. But you have no idea what kind of people the three Xia brothers are. Just imagine three criminals coming and going from this house, calling themselves your uncles. I cannot accept that while I'm alive. What would happen to the two of you if I die? I think the intermediary today was sent by the three brothers. But I could only address those words to her."

Because of my selfishness, my instinct for self-protection, and because of the extreme notoriety of the three brothers, after hearing Mother's explanation I imagined three hungry vultures swooping down upon two helpless chickens, while the mother hen, her feathers standing on end, was ready to put up a desperate fight. I thought about Mother's scholarly family background and forgave her for her cruel words.

We were wandering refugees after the outbreak of the Pacific War, and missed our hometown badly. One day, Mother decided that we should sneak back home and try to live there a few days. She would rather risk living at home than bear the suffering of being homeless.

The ancient village had fallen into the hands of the Japanese fascist army, which relied on a "peace-keeping association" to control the situation. We returned at nightfall and snuck into a room upstairs. Nobody knew of our arrival save a few close relatives and friends who visited us through secret arrangements. Only at night, behind secured doors, did Sister and I dare make any sounds at all. We roamed the grounds of our home in darkness, feeling happier here than in the metropolis. Sometimes we were even so bold as to break into our own garden where pavilions, scholars' rocks, and the pond were bathed in such bright moonlight that the place seemed hardly changed from its daytime existence. It was so pleasant that we decided to invite Mother to share our roamings with us. We ran to our upstairs room, sweating and panting, and told Mother how much fun it was revisiting the garden. Mother said with a broad smile, "Well, you sound as if you've broken into the Emperor's Garden. Tomorrow night I'll go, too, and we'll bring some food and wine so that we can enjoy the moon."

We washed ourselves and spied on the table a volume of *The Complete Collection of Tang Poems*. Mother began to teach us how to read Du Fu's *qiyan*- and *wuyan*-style poems. We knitted our brows, pretending we were moved so that Mother wouldn't feel so lonely. Mother looked at us, closed the book, and brought us a box of cakes and biscuits that were local delicacies. We could appreciate these treats more than Tang poetry.

For a while Mr. Lu, our housekeeper, seemed full of cares, rising early, retiring late, rushing to the gate with our four male servants to find out who was ringing the doorbell. If he needed to go out, Mr. Lu would always return when he said he would. If he was going to be even a little late, he would send someone home so that Mother wouldn't worry.

We had returned home at the end of summer and delighted in the scenery of autumn in our garden. Soon it was the end of the year. Cold, heavy snow fell for several days. Sister became ill, and I felt numb with the gunshots and the exploding bombs around us—the usual New Year's atmosphere nonexistent. I sat beside Sister on her bed as she lay breathing heavily and wished that I were sick, too.

One afternoon, Mr. Lu tiptoed upstairs and beckoned me. I quietly followed him downstairs and learned that Xia Mingzhu was dead! How could that be? Mr. Lu avoided my stare and said with his head turned sideways, "I have to tell your mother in person."

"No, tell me in detail. I'll know how to tell her."

"It'd be better if I told her. I also need to consult with her about some matters. Why don't you go upstairs? Wait until she wakes up from her nap and has had her tea. Then you come to the window and I'll meet her next to the plants in the yard."

I went up and found Mother already in the bathroom washing her face. As soon as she finished, I told her that Mr. Lu wanted to see her about something. Mother thought it was about the usual business of shopping for the New Year, so she mumbled, "It has to somewhat be like a New Year."

I walked to the window and waved to Mr. Lu who stood in the snow alone, his shoulders covered with white powder. He quickly approached Mother and said without the usual initial courtesies, "I learned yesterday that the Japanese Kempeitai arrested Miss Xia on the pretext that she played 'La Marseillaise' on the piano. When the head of the Kempeitai saw her, he suspected she was a spy. They had a poor translator, so they deliberately asked her in English. She fell for it and defended herself in fluent English. This plus her appearance, her European style of dress, confirmed to them that she was a spy from England or America. They tortured her, and then tried to rape her that night. Miss Xia slapped the Japanese soldier and the beast cut off her hand with his sword. Miss Xia knew it was hopeless and cursed Japan for invading China. He then sliced off one of her arms.... I looked for the three Xia brothers, but they've all fled.... Her body was thrown into the snow.... I saw the body myself, it's afternoon now, perhaps when it gets dark, I think...."

I wanted to help. Mr. Lu needed my mother to tell him to retrieve the body, and I made a decision right then that if Mother didn't grant her permission, I would kneel down to plead, and if pleading failed I would threaten her.

I looked Mother directly in the eye and she gazed back at me. Tears streamed down her face. I didn't have to kneel; I guessed wrong. How could I have even thought of threatening her?

Mother calmed down, took out a handkerchief to wipe her tears, and said, "Mr. Lu, could you please see that a coffin is prepared for the body? Make sure to gather her whole body. But we have to move quickly. Once you have ordered a coffin, wait until dark and bring a few people to help. Make sure no one sees you. Don't be careless. We cannot afford another tragedy."

I knew that Mr. Lu could get everything done properly. He set off to carry out Mother's instructions when she shouted, "Wait!," and rushed upstairs. Even though I knew Mr. Lu was in charge of all our financial affairs, I still thought that Mother was going to get money.

But instead she returned with a gray overcoat and a dark flannel hat.

"Wrap her in this overcoat. Tuck her hair into the hat. Buy bedding and a quilt. The rest you know, follow our customs. But skip the wake rituals. Bury her immediately. Bury her in our ancestral graveyard. Don't level the grave. We'll have a tombstone made for her in the future."

As Sister was sick, Mother told me not to tell her just

yet. "When you children can wander out safely, go together to visit her grave."

After Miss Xia was buried, Mother sent Mr. Lu to look for the little girl who wanted to be part of our family.

A few days later, Mr. Lu reported that she had been sold and nobody knew where she was taken.

An Empty Room

AS THE MOUNTAIN crested its slope steepened. I was already sweating. A church appeared at the top of the crest. I thought I should rest there a bit before deciding when to descend.

The war had just ended. The church was deserted. The altar, tables, and chairs had long been removed. Only the holy statue remained—Christ's face, covered with dust, revealed an extraordinary quality of steadfast perseverance. Half the keys of an old piano still made a kind of grating sound. If someone could've composed a piece to fit its condition, that would've been very interesting indeed.

Was there anything else worth seeing? Why was I the only one hiking? Winter days in the mountains were dead with creeks dried and bamboo barely green.

Walking through a bamboo forest, I found another path to descend.

Then through the twists and turns of the path I glimpsed a temple. If there were monks we could have tea together, I thought to myself. I had decided to hike alone as I was weary of the crowded city, but as I had yet to come across anyone, an unexpected chat with a monk would be nice.

The gate was open. Fallen leaves in the yard and dust floating in the hall indicated that this was another place in ruins. The temple was more appealing than the church, though. The corridors crisscrossed and the tall ancient trees provided heavy shade so that even in decay there was a tranquil beauty. Behind the main hall stood a two-story building. I called out a few times but received no response. I walked upstairs to look around. Two of the three rooms didn't have doors, their dilapidated wooden walls exposed within. Empty, empty. I came to the third room and found a screen door ajar. I pushed it open but withdrew my hand immediately—a sudden flood of pink washed over me. The walls inside were painted the color of flowering cherry blossoms. I felt a "human presence," but after a quick inspection it was clear that this room, too, was empty. The walls, however, were freshly painted with a clean evenness. No furniture. The floor was covered with pieces of paper and piles of empty Kodak boxes. Stepping on the paper scraps, I felt as if a rich carpet covered the entire floor.

1. This couldn't possibly be a room for monks since the walls were pink.

2. The previous tenants must have been a young couple, possibly newlyweds.

3. They were photographers or lovers of photography.

4. They had taken residence here recently and left not too long before I arrived.

These speculations seemed disconnected from the temporal and spatial dimensions of the war and of this remote mountainous region. The war had lasted eight long years. Did they come here for refuge? Was it possible that they really had the leisure time to paint the walls and take photos? Where could they have found food in the mountains? If they had no money, they couldn't have lived here long. If they did have money, they would have been robbed. Even Erich Remarque's wartime lovebirds wouldn't choose such an eerie, ancient temple.

I picked up some of the papers and could see they were letters. Scanning the papers on the ground I could see that all the pages were letters. Why so many letters? There was no order to the strewn pages and thus the letters were more difficult to understand than the most absurd novels. It was clear, however, that the missives were written between a man and a woman. The man's name was Liang—"darling Liang," "my Liang," "your Liang." The woman's name was Mei—"dearest Mei," "my Mei forever." They wrote all about love, the twists and turns of their love together, in a style befitting college-educated liberal arts majors.

I was frustrated. Sitting amidst the stacks of papers, my legs began to itch from flea bites. That there were so many fleas suggested that someone had inhabited the room. My head pounded and my cheeks burned from reading the letters. The setting sun tinted the windowsills orange; the evening wind vigorously shook the bare branches. I would need to hike down the mountain quickly.

I inspected the walls and corners one last time and found no bloodstains or bullet holes. The door and windows weren't damaged. Every Kodak box was empty. Every paper scrap was a sheet from a letter. Yet I could find no envelopes. Was it possible this was a film set? But that would hardly make sense as the letters contained real substance. I couldn't take away all the pages, so I removed my scarf and wrapped up a large bundle. Then I stuffed my pockets with a few Kodak boxes and rushed downstairs. Circling the temple, I could find nothing else of note. There still wasn't a single person in sight. The surrounding wilderness now frightened me. I descended with the letters like a woodcutter carrying his firewood.

For the next several days I read the letters and formulated this loose sketch from the chaos: Liang and Mei had been in love for a long time. Both their families strongly objected to the match. Liang, out of despair, repeatedly wrote that being dead was better than being alive. Mei asked him not to take his life so lightly and said that his first priority should be his own career and future. She confessed that her own days living in this world were numbered. The rest was more or less intensely passionate yet somewhat empty expressions of love. It was also strange that letters from both of them were dated with the month but not the year. Neither spoke of the war's tragedies. It was as if love had nothing to do with time and war. As the letters weren't literature after all, the words became tiresome.

I reasoned again with a list:

1. If they had lived together in the temple room, they wouldn't have left without the letters.

2. If Liang had lived there alone, it was puzzling that his letters to Mei were mixed with Mei's letters to him.

3. If Mei had died first and she had returned her letters to Liang before her death, then Liang would have cherished these letters and would not have scattered them around so carelessly.

4. If, after Mei's death, Liang killed himself because he was heartbroken, then he would have destroyed the letters before he committed suicide rather than risking their discovery by gossiping strangers.

5. If they had chosen a ritual Japanese suicide—jumping off the mountain together or throwing themselves into a fire—then Liang still would've burned the letters before their death. This would be the only way to insure a clean break from the world.

6. Perhaps Liang was murdered and was robbed of everything save these useless letters. But then why would the criminals bother to leave the letters and not the envelopes?

7. If Liang had been arrested for political reasons, these letters would've been confiscated by the authorities as valuable evidence.

I was too young then to have sufficient reasoning capacities, but I did reach one definite conclusion: when I found the letters, Liang and Mei were no longer in this world. After my discovery, I moved several times and lost the letters. I've never had the chance to return to the room. None of the cases of murder and robbery reported in newspapers mentioned Liang or Mei or anything similar to what I saw in the temple. I've since met others with the same name but no one was the Liang or Mei I knew.

A few decades have passed since then. I still remember the surprise I felt when I first pushed open that screen door. The desolate winter scenery of the mountain, the abandoned church and temple as if the whole of humanity had disappeared, contrasted strikingly with the flowering cherry blossoms that blazed before me—people, life ... bluish-white letterhead, golden yellow Kodak boxes—it was like the welcome of spring, or an unexpected encounter with an old friend.

Those fleas that had bitten Liang may have also bitten Mei. A poet once compared the blood of a man and a woman mixed within the living walls of a flea to a marriage temple. What a refined sentiment of tragedy! By coincidence my own blood was mixed in as well, though I was innocent. I never witnessed the marriage of Liang and Mei.

I record this story in memory of my youth. And still cannot comprehend what it means—which only demonstrates that I haven't made much progress these past few decades.

Fong Fong No. 4

FONG FONG was my niece's classmate. My niece had mentioned her quite a few times before she introduced her to me. Fong Fong was quite shy. Her frail build was a stark contrast to my niece's healthy glow but they didn't seem to mind. There was no need for me to play host with them so they came and went as they pleased and soon Fong Fong was no stranger. I secretly thought of her as one of my piano students. Both she and my niece were quite advanced musicians.

I'm only four years older than my niece—her youngest uncle. Talking with her and Fong Fong wasn't any different from conversing with my other friends. And despite the gender difference, they dragged me along to shop for dresses and shoes as they respected my opinions in such matters. We casually strolled from store to store, idling away that wondrous phase of life called youth.

Ding Yan was a young man who was a decent pianist, though he made rather slow progress in his lessons with me twice a week. I had long sensed that he was in love with Fong Fong.

The summer came when my niece was admitted to the Central Academy of Music in Beijing. She left Shanghai laughing and crying. Fong Fong wasn't accepted and stayed behind. She mentioned something about finding a job.

As time passed, Fong Fong still visited often. I didn't know if this was Ding Yan's idea or hers. After his lesson, Ding Yan would chat with Fong Fong while I busied myself with little chores.

The next summer Ding Yan was accepted by the Shanghai Academy of Music. I was happy for him. He and Fong Fong would visit together and we'd all listen to music and cook. There were no more piano lessons, just meandering conversations between friends. My niece returned from the north and stayed with me, adding to the lively atmosphere. Who could've guessed that Fong Fong actually had no romantic interest in Ding Yan.

"It's quite simple," my niece told me. "She doesn't like him at all. His letters to her are heated. But the more passion he expresses, the more it makes her laugh. She showed me all his letters."

"Please stop! What are you two laughing at? I think Fong Fong is misleading him. You shouldn't read those letters anymore. Ding Yan has very fine qualities, though perhaps he isn't handsome enough for her?"

"Why ask me? I'm not the one receiving the letters."

"Didn't the two of you laugh at his slender build? Or poke fun at his thin neck?"

"It's seems as if you've been eavesdropping on us. Fong Fong isn't the person Ding Yan imagines her to be."

To be fair I'd say Fong Fong herself wasn't exactly a stunning beauty. She was a bit too thin with a somewhat plain appearance but did have pretty eyes. It's possible she thought too highly of herself.

Ding Yan fell ill when he learned about Fong Fong's complete lack of interest in him. "It was all a dream," he said to me after recovering. "I bear no grudge nor resentment. It was just my imagination that deceived me."

I found his words quite noble and praised him. "I may have taught you piano but I could never have taught you this lesson. You're obviously your own teacher—and no nightingale from the nineteenth century."

My words brought tears to his eyes. His love was genuine, and unreciprocated for such a long time, reminding me of certain occurrences in my own past.

Whether it was because Fong Fong wanted to avoid Ding Yan or because she was eager to establish her independence, she too moved to Beijing and became a copy editor at a publishing house. Ding Yan rarely stopped by, and my place became lifeless. Others visited but it wasn't the same.

Fong Fong often wrote me letters on elegant paper sealed in matching envelopes. There was a graceful flow in

her handwriting and a cleverness in her choice of words—
cleverness because her deliberate turns in idioms and
phrases formed elusive images and a charming uncertainty
in meaning. If you had never met her before, from her letters you'd think she was an eloquent and refined woman.
It's also possible that if her words weren't written in such
fine calligraphy, her letters might not have seemed as graceful. When did she start practicing calligraphy anyway? This
practice seemed quite incompatible with her person—her
slightly rigid manners and her relatively common speech.
And yet she was a gifted letter writer. In my replies, I tried
to be playful and imitate her style of mixing archaic and
contemporary diction. Fortunately, I didn't have to worry
about "love" as I believed in love at first sight. Without this
initial spark of love, you could see the person every day and
still not feel anything. Ding Yan asked about Fong Fong
and I showed him her letters. He was also impressed with
her calligraphy.

Our correspondence, or rather our word games, became
a regular ritual. Then one autumn I was invited to Beijing to sit on a judging panel for a piano competition. I
wrote to my niece and Fong Fong, not expecting that they
would ask me to purchase some winter and spring clothes
for them. Besides being a little awkward for a man to buy
women's clothes, they didn't even tell me their sizes. So I
made my best guess and purchased a few things.

After they tried on the clothes, they were, to my surprise, quite happy with my selections. "But *please* spare me

such responsibilities in the future," I said.

My job as a judge was easy enough, nodding when everyone else voiced praise and nodding again when they criticized. None of my students were part of the competition so I could afford to be relaxed. Still, somehow word spread that I was fair, mature, and even showed depth as a judge. Nobody, though, knew how my niece, Fong Fong, and I played on the swings and slides in Tao-Ren-Ting Children's Park, or how, afterward, we competed to see who could eat the most dumplings and how I emerged the winner. Nobody saw our childlike innocence.

All the other memories of my visit to the capital that year are now vague. What I do distinctly remember is receiving a letter from Fong Fong at my hotel, though of course we were both in Beijing. In the letter she wrote, among other things, "You looked so handsome in that leather hat yesterday!"

I didn't particularly appreciate her flattering tone of voice, so I wore a different hat the next time we met.

After I returned home, our correspondence gradually became less frequent. Her letters then began to arrive from An-hui Province where she had been sent to do farm work. The playful naughtiness in her lines vanished. Occasionally, she would include phrases such as "years pass by like a river ... alas, the flower-like beauty of women ..." I didn't laugh, as I, too, needed to work extremely hard just to put food on the table, leaving me with no leisurely feelings. Things continued in this way and two more years disappeared.

As Fong Fong's family lived in Shanghai, her trip home
for Spring Festival was already long overdue. Then she
suddenly showed up at my place one afternoon and announced that she had been home for more than a week. I
was astonished—it was as if she had changed into another
person. While we caught up, I secretly studied the new full-
ness of her body: her skin was a light tan suffused in pink;
a touch of rural resilience complemented her fragile build;
her manners were no longer rigid; her body revealed the
curves of a country girl. The years of farm work must have
shaped her figure, plus nature, home cooking, and whatever else added to a belated youthfulness. Her eyes, already
her most striking aspect, now cast vivacious glances that
brightened her whole face. This was without a doubt a
very attractive woman. I began to feel a different kind of
harmony between us, as if we were both more sophisti-
cated. Her speech was more fluent, more akin to her flowing calligraphy.

With a twinge of regret, I thought to myself, What if she
were like this when we had first met?

Anyone who believes that a whole-hearted devotion is
invincible in love is completely mistaken! Physical attrac-
tion is so powerful a factor that sometimes you are swayed
to swallow your words of rage in silence. Virtuous deeds,
sorrowful pleas, and other such things are really not re-
lated to love, though they might bring you a small dose of
sympathy and respect, and though you might even want
to construct these acts into something you call love. But

this concoction can't intoxicate you nor your beloved. It will turn sour and bitter and become something you must push away. Or perhaps you won't know if you should push it away or drink it. Love isn't a universal fact recognized by all. It isn't a treasure the world has rarely seen. It simply means that the one I love is the one who intoxicates me. A homely appearance is beautiful when it enchants you. Lovers have unique eyes and hearts, and think: "No one but me can see my love." What else makes us happier than feelings of pride and confidence in love?

Yet I soon cooled my heart. Even though we had known each other for five years and had written each other many letters immersed in elusiveness, I knew nothing of her intentions. I knew she wasn't hypocritical or pretentious. But indifference, timidity, and a slight self-centeredness also added to her personality. I visited her at her parents' home a few times and sensed that she offered only half her heart, or a quarter of it, to her parents and siblings. Her interest in music and literature was cursory at best. It wasn't that she never did anything wholeheartedly; it was as if the Creator had given her this half-or-quarter of a heart. I somehow felt consoled by this small sense of fatalism.

Another letter from Fong Fong while we were both in the same city—she could somehow enhance her elegance with stamps.

This letter I read over and over again, my initial surprise turning into ecstasy. The end of it read: "Even if I wasn't in love with you before, I long promised myself that I would be yours. As I fear this letter may arrive a day too late, I've chosen the day after tomorrow, the 24th, which happens to be Christmas Eve. I'll come and stay through Christmas. So this is it. When we meet, it's not that we need to speak but that we don't need to speak. I love you, I am yours, the day after tomorrow at six in the evening. I guess no need to ring the doorbell."

If I had held to my principles, I would have felt my pride injured. How could she be so confident of possessing Christmas Eve? That she loved me didn't mean that I loved her. I was merely on the receiving end; she was making a rendezvous with herself. "I am yours" she wrote, but didn't I deserve a chance to say "I am yours," too? What did she expect?

But none of this crossed my mind at the time. I only felt unexpected excitement. She wasn't the Fong Fong I had known for so many years: usually detached, an observer, evasive, someone who feared fire and water, a non-adventurer who never bothered to explore further.... Yet, all of a sudden she was decisive and enthusiastic, her voice insistent and clear.... These contradictions only intensified my sense of triumph at the time. I seemed to be the one who had won, so much so that I was almost apologetic: What merits did I have to entice her in this way?

I turned down Christmas invitations from friends, cleaned the living room, bedroom, and bathroom, bought flowers, wine, and sweet and savory foods....

It was six. She arrived. The doorbell didn't ring.

Fong Fong wasn't dressed any differently. Her eyes, her voice, her smile weren't that different either. Our dinner was quiet and simple. We weren't sure what to say after we ate. I almost thought we'd drink our tea and smoke our cigarettes till late in the night and I would, as usual, walk her to the bus stop.

Did Adam and Eve first make love in the dark? Do all the ardent acts of love depend on the darkness? When the lights switched off, she suddenly became that person she described in her letter, the one who loved me and was mine. I repeated her name softly a few times; she replied and then motioned for me to stop. As I was about to pour out a surge of words from my heart, she fell asleep. I didn't close my eyes until the break of dawn, and then pretended I had just woken up so that I could speak to her as she rose from bed.

When she returned from the bathroom, she sat on the chair and stared at the lowered blinds.

I quickly got up and made some breakfast. As the fear of leaving her alone grew, I walked over to kiss her but she pushed me away.

I wondered if the glimpse of dawn through the blinds made her shy. I approached her again, but she stood up and said, "It's time I went home."

Then I saw the indifference in her face. Anxiety gripped me: "Don't leave, please!"

"I have to leave."

"But ... when will you come back?"

She shook her head.

"What is it?"

"Nothing."

"Did I do something wrong?"

"Please ... don't start."

She didn't want me to see her off. Fong Fong opened the door and closed it behind her, then descended the stairs.

Five to six, Christmas morning.

I can imagine the remorse an alcoholic feels after getting drunk, followed by the temporary resolution to quit. I don't think it was absurd that Fong Fong wanted an ephemeral happiness. Nor do I think we made a mistake. There was obviously something she wasn't telling me but, still, there was no reason for her to leave like that even if she didn't want to stay together.

For two days I didn't hear from her. I went to her home and was told that she had returned to Anhui. I later learned that she had headed further north. I don't remember who told me that.

I didn't gain anything from her loss and she didn't gain anything from my loss. It was as if I had found a ring in a dream and then lost it in the same dream.

A riddle. I tried to search through the rules of human emotions, the wide range of varying rules, but could find no answers and so I suffered.

The suffering of searching for an answer in vain....There is no way to continue searching if the suffering continues. Gradually the picture became even more blurry.

Great misfortunes often descend without warning. The first two years of the Ten-Year-Catastrophe were unbearably painful as I watched several colleagues in our music circle disappear one after another, until trouble unexpectedly found me. Without getting into too much detail, what followed was a long, dark period of feeling neither dead nor alive. Two fingers on my right hand and one finger on my left hand were broken, and the Catastrophe finally ended. Once again I was invited on judging panels. Does this prove the proverbial wisdom of "affirmation at the end of negation"? I was even elected Secretary General of the Municipal Association of Musicians. Dignitaries of all kinds floated toward me with smiling faces and flattering words. Yet my home was the same place; I was still my same single self. Every day the same morning passed into the same evening.

Then one evening the doorbell rang. After fourteen years I still recognized Fong Fong's voice.

Her thinning hair was turning gray, and her loud talking echoed in the hallway without pause, though I could barely understand what she was saying. She was dressed in the northern style from head to foot—from the back I could have never guessed who she was. I showed her to the living room to sit and turned on another light so that I could look at her more closely. Her eyes, mouth, and nose were somehow shrunken. Her high and slightly wrinkled forehead I had never seen before. It was drizzling outside as it always is in March in Shanghai, but her face seemed to be covered with dust. She looked withered, even her clothing looked withered.

Her voice grew in intensity. I listened without much comprehension, watching her high forehead and trying to think of a way to relax her so that we could talk more slowly, more meaningfully.

Her words didn't stop: "Ten years is how long it has taken for me to return ... two children ... yes, boys ... it took me all these years to be able to return to Shanghai ... he didn't come this time ... yes, he works in a food and goods co-op in Harbin and travels everywhere for supplies ... I'm the accountant of course ... very busy ... I'll give you the address so do write me ... I went to the Musicians' Congress ... sorry, Association ... the first thing that my brother and sister told me when I came home is that you are one of the three most prominent celebrities in Shanghai ... I also read it in the paper ... your name is often in the paper ... you don't look old, still your former self ... how is it that you haven't aged ... ten years ... more than ten years ... when I returned to Anhui, they didn't want me anymore, so I tried Changchun then Shenyang, then finally settled down in Harbin ... my oldest child is eight, the younger one six ... my husband wants a girl, but I don't ... my sister wanted to come with me, but I lied to her and said I was going to the train station...."

Tea was ready. She rose to take the cup before I could put it on the table. She sipped it like a northern peasant would sip it, sucking the water loudly. Then her voice continued:

"So you are one of the three most prominent celebrities ... yesterday, I went to the Association yesterday, and the guard at the gate gave me your address. Actually, I had looked for you there before and thought you had moved, or had died during the political campaign ... too many died ... I have moved around so much, spent six months in Dalian ... you don't look old at all, you look the same, strange you don't even have white hair ... the guard said that I should find you soon, that you are going abroad? England? France? Are you coming back? I doubt it. You aren't old ... I wasn't free yesterday and had to do some shopping today ... I'm leaving, too, so I had to find you tonight. I was worried even as I stepped through your doorway ... oh, tea, let me take that ..."

I tried to calm her down. Only if she was calm could she remember. I served some snacks with the tea, then brought out a few newly printed, signed musical scores and an album of personal photographs. I tried to prolong the intermission, hoping her thoughts would connect to the Fong Fong of the past, and thus to my own past self. The doorbell rang. Too many unexpected visitors. Three self-important men entered.

Fong Fong put away my gifts and with one gulp finished her tea.

"I shouldn't bother you," she said. "I'm leaving now. I'm so happy to have found you. I'm leaving. Please don't get up."

I asked for her address. She wrote it down while reading it out loud.

I followed her downstairs to the door. Her hands were rough and bony. She walked extremely fast. Before I could say anything, she disappeared into the crowded street. The road glistened with rain, though it had already stopped raining.

After the three visitors left, I read her address carefully in the light. I could see traces of her old handwriting that I imagined only my eyes could detect.

There would be another strange encounter. Not in the form of her person, but in the form of a letter.

"It was quite unexpected that I should see you again," she wrote. "I thought you could never have survived the persecution. I thought that as soon as I returned home to Shanghai, my family would tell me about your death. I was shocked to hear you were still alive. You don't even look old. I'm very happy for you. How difficult it must have been those long years. You mustn't worry yourself as your life was saved. Your health is important.

"I decided to travel by ship to Dalian and connect to a train. It's quieter and cheaper this way. I hadn't seen the ocean for a long time. The Bohai Sea may not be the greatest sea but it's still infinitely vast. I stood on deck, alone, looking at the blue ocean and the blue sky and the white sea gulls gliding along. I cried with regret, having left you so abruptly. It is much too late for regret, so my regret grows even more. I've cried nearly every day since then.

"Will you write to me when you are settled abroad? Thank you for the photographs, the ones of our good times in Beijing. Thank you also for the musical scores. I could even read some of them. You are a fine composer. I'm tempted to try them out on the piano.

"If you return to China in the future, please let me know. I simply would like to know and wouldn't bother you. But if you ever come to Harbin, please don't forget to visit my family.

"Take care of yourself when you're in that foreign land! I wish you the best in everything!"

At the end of the letter she wrote out her full address again. It was astonishing that she who had become so worn and chatty could still write a letter like that. Her handwriting had declined. The paper was a crude kind of letterhead from their co-op.

I wrote to her before I left China, informing her of my date of departure and my country of destination. I didn't say a word about our past as some things seem clearer if not openly clarified. I only wrote:

"I was also happy to see you again, and I thank you for thinking of me and wishing me well as you stood on deck before the sky and sea. I'll certainly return, and will visit Harbin. I used to visit Harbin often. 'Dao-li,' inside the rails, is prettier than 'Dao-wai,' outside the rails. The Songhua River and Sun Island are utterly charming. Please tell your two lovely sons that an uncle wants to meet them and take them duck-hunting in the reed marshes."

As I was busy attending farewell parties, packing, and preparing travel documents, Fong Fong's letter calmed me. Our relationship was no longer about love.; it was no longer about virtue. It was simply the light of gratitude in the soul that refuses to die out. The agony of being an atheist is that in the moment you feel moved toward the divine, you simply cannot reach your hands up to God. So just as I was about to offer my hands up in gratitude I had to withdraw them and absorb the gratitude inside me. Nobody would be there to receive it anyway.

Another strange encounter. It arrived not in the form of a letter but in the form of the wind. After I had visited the Tower of London, I walked along the Thames with a heavy heart. As I watched the strong wind tear through people's hair and clothes, a cold thought crossed my mind:

If I had died during the Catastrophe, if I had killed myself or had been killed, with my good name destroyed, what would Fong Fong have thought when she returned home and heard that from her family? Perhaps she would put on an it-has-nothing-to-do-with-me look, then pretend to let out a sigh of sympathy before assuming the it-has-nothing-to-do-with-me look again. She would secretly congratulate herself, "I was lucky to have left him in the first place. I was lucky not to have turned back. Otherwise, I would have been implicated. Even if I wasn't killed, I would have suffered inconceivable consequences. I was smart and completely right in my choice. What a narrow escape!"

This uneasy thought followed me persistently. An old Chinese friend of mine had been a longtime resident of London. We could talk about anything together. He is a literary man, intelligent and kind-hearted, a devout humanist. We were both half drunk one night, and I told him about the four phases of Fong Fong, sparing no detail. I wanted to hear his thoughts about my uneasy encounter with the wind. Immediately after I finished the story, he exclaimed, "How could you have such thoughts!"

Then, a silent pause later he said, "Tomorrow, we will discuss this tomorrow."

"Why wait until tomorrow?" I chuckled. "Are you going to lose sleep over my thoughts? Don't tell me you're going to consult some reference books?"

"I admit I'm confused," he laughed. "You and Fong Fong are ordinary people, but this situation concerns a complex issue. Montaigne wouldn't be able to offer an answer even if you could ask him. Let me think about it—I don't want to give you a wrong answer."

We met in a café the following day. My friend looked serious indeed and burst out without warning, "Your thoughts seem completely accurate!"

His loud voice alarmed two ladies sitting at a nearby table. I apologized on his behalf. My literary friend said, "You don't need to apologize. I would rather like it if they heard this story from your past."

"Shhh ... Europeans are quite innocent of this sort of thing."

Notes from Underground

I FIRST MET HIM *at his art opening in Boston in 1985. Then ten years later, under unexpected circumstances, I finally learned about his "notes." He invited me to visit him in his apartment in the suburbs of New York one winter evening and brought me to his study. His manuscript was stacked next to his lamp on his desk— sixty-six handwritten pages on thin rice paper that had yellowed; the red-stamped letterhead indicating a certain work unit that existed during those times which I too experienced. Each piece of paper was filled on both sides with tiny, graceful words handwritten in blue ink. A feeling akin to religious awe washed over me, though I'm not religious, nor is the artist. He explained to me that that the manuscript was composed as a story in the style of prose-poetry, but that he now calls it his "notes." It would be difficult to restore the story as a whole, considering the pages weren't numbered in the first place and much of the writing was faded to a point that it was impossible to discern. I persuaded him to let me transcribe a few selected paragraphs so that he could pass on to* posterity some evidence of his resilient spirit and preserve a part of our historical memory that is fading faster than the blue ink on the thin sheets.

The story of how the author was locked in an underground prison and how he was able to write the "notes" is remarkable. His underground is not a basement in nineteenth-century St. Petersburg but one in twentieth-century China. The prison was an abandoned air-raid shelter in Shanghai where our author was confined as a solitary prisoner for ten months from 1971 to 1972. As terrifying as this may sound today, it was one of many illegal prisons in those days and he was one of many "prisoners" whose "crime" was belonging to a certain "undesirable class" (in his case, he was classified as an "intellectual with decadent thoughts"). Such people were imprisoned without trial, without sentencing, without a court of law. This period of Chinese history seems too complex for foreigners, or even subsequent generations in China born after the 1960s, to truly comprehend. For it is extraordinarily difficult to explain certain phenomena that were common then. Suffice it to say that the artist experienced the kind of imprisonment which was imposed on him by "rebels" (zaofanpai) in his work unit. The charges against him: "dangerous and decadent thoughts."

So for ten months the artist was confined underground, in an abandoned air-raid shelter flooded with dirty water, dwelling in total darkness save for a dim gasoline lamp. His immediate family had died and his remaining relatives thought he was dead. Those who left him in this underground hole provided him with paper so that he could write down and submit his "confessions." He secretly used some of the sheets to write his book. He then carefully *folded the manuscript and sewed it into his cotton-padded winter pants to avoid detection. Then, one day, he was released, and miraculously he walked out in those pants, with the manuscript intact.*

The artist's reasons for writing the "notes" are personal. But he did reveal one thing to me: "It was my way to stay alive." The following are a few excerpts from his "notes."

I. Death of a Diva

It's ironic that in this dungeon, forced into the life of an ascetic, I should feel like St. Anthony. As long as I can mentally resist the temptation of illusions, I will have my respite; yet I know that another storm will come, and that the punishment will continue, so that in the future when I remember the here and now, I might even call it the "good old days." In front of me is a dark blue inkbottle and a gray ashtray made of fine china. The ink bottle is provided by the work unit. Being public property, it is perhaps "socialist" in nature. The ashtray used to be a sugar bowl, part of a tea set made in England that I brought here with me. I guess that makes it "capitalist" in nature. When I first came to the dungeon I would smoke a pack of cigarettes a day; recently I have cut down to half a pack. With a wave of my hand, the matchstick with which I light my cigarette goes out. This, I discovered some time ago, could be used for my entertainment. All I had to do was plant the stick gently into the ashes in the ashtray and watch it burn from top to bottom, a tiny bright-red pillar of flame. The pillar would then turn gray, bend, break, and become a circle of ash among ashes. For several months I have been successfully directing the same drama: the ashtray resembles a circular stage on which the matchstick, like a legendary diva, sings her swan song before she slowly falls to the ground and dies.

II. People on the Road

I enjoy watching men and women silently walking on the road, their faces expressionless, their attention undivided. A person on the road seems absorbed in self-respect, as if he would explode at the slightest provocation. His carefree look is but a façade behind which his instincts stand on guard. That he is on the road means he is in "transition"—he could have just come from doing something, or he could be on his way to do something, or perhaps what he has to do requires his attention in two separate places. Thus he is between one thing and another thing, which is a state of neither good nor evil. You cannot say with certainty whether a passerby is good or evil; he embodies the concept of "human." But when he (or she) meets someone he knows, when he says hello, then stops and makes conversation, all of a sudden he is transformed from a conceptual human to a specific human with his own individuality. When the two part ways again, he promptly reassumes the identity of a "passerby." It now seems conceivable that the thing he is going to do could be good or bad, or that he has just done something good or bad. But since he is on the road and is no longer involved, it is still difficult to say if he is good or if he is bad. Since I am imprisoned, I no longer have the pleasure of watching people walking on the road. My connections with the world have been reduced to such a minimal degree that even if I were on the road I could only see but not talk. I have no need to cherish the memories of any relatives or friends. So I devote my nostalgia to men and women endlessly walking on boulevards and in streets, innocent of good and evil. Whether their past or their future is good or bad is unknown to me and of no concern.

III. Tiny Tassels

Life can drive the young to hopelessness as it can drive the middle-aged to hopelessness, but who grieves more in their hopelessness? It would seem that the youth would grieve more, but it is the middle-aged person who really gives up and no longer dreams. Because hope is the premise for life, hope will endure in the subconscious if it is destroyed in the conscious mind. In this way the life of humans can be distinguished from the life of animals. The hopelessness of animals is a biological and instinctive feeling of the end, but the hopelessness of humans is a final judgment based on reason and conscious thought. A young person retains more of the animalistic quality, while a person aware of aging is being transformed to a "human being" in a purer sense; he is learning precisely those fatal points that render hope hopeless. I don't have the good fortune of living in the nineteenth century. But I once saw a picture of the room in which Lermontov was imprisoned: there was a round table covered with a thick, solid tablecloth, a table lamp with an opalescent glass shade, a brass teakettle, and two high-back chairs. The poet-prisoner, in his military uniform, was allowed to receive visitors, such as Belinsky. If I had lived in Lermontov's times, I wouldn't have been thrown into this dungeon flooded with filthy water. I feel profoundly relieved that Lermontov was more fortunate than me—Lermontov with his teakettle so authentically Russian, and his tablecloth with its rows of tiny tassels hanging from the sides.

IV. Who Is Truly Fearless?

"I have not yet loved you in the way it's expressed in music"—suddenly I remember these words. Now that I'm in prison, I cannot possibly find Wagner's original text, although I believe this is more or less what he said. Music is a form of art constituted by its own vanishings. In its essence and depth music is thus closest to "death." Before I turn forty I have no plan to write my memoirs, but I'm quite impressed with Rousseau's late work *Reveries of the Solitary Walker*. Turgenev's *Literary Memoir* is so slim a book that I once thought it couldn't be a must-read. But it turned out to be utterly engaging. As for myself, I still follow Flaubert's advice: "Reveal art; conceal the artist." When catastrophe sweeps through your political life, economic condition, love life, or your pursuit of art, you are reduced to a miserable and ridiculous state of existence. Your patience and endurance are not enough for you to overcome the adversity. Consequently, you are forced into the underground, that is you have to fight even if you don't want to (as you must live to avoid death). Mayakovsky was forced into such a desperate situation that he had no other option but suicide. Before he took his own life, he had to fake the failure of love as his reason, saying that "a small boat of love runs up on the rock of life." He was neither a collectivist nor an individualist. A thorough individualist fears nothing. As far as my feelings about the world are concerned, I will say, in Wagner's words: "I have not yet loved you in the way it's expressed in music."

V. Happiness

"Why is it that some humans are Persians?" It was Montesquieu who asked this most interesting question. Mérimée then asked: "Why is it that some humans are Spanish?" So he went to Spain and wrote his letters and travelogues that described bullfighting, robbery, and the death penalty. His doubts vanished. But what question am I left with? I

venture the view that "happiness" is so esoteric a body of
knowledge that it virtually cannot be articulated. It is a
trick that you can perfect only through trials and tribu-
lations. From such examples as the facial make-up techniques of the ancient Egyptians, the schools for training
prostitutes in ancient Greece, the design and display of bedrooms in ancient Arabia, and the all too exquisite body language of ancient India, it seems that humanity has tried to
create "happiness" and manipulate it. Historians have con-
strued such stories as "golden ages" or "prosperous periods,"
but they have compiled no record of any specific "happy
individuals." An individual who knows what happiness is
and is good at it is a genius. The genius of happiness is not
an innate genius but a product of deliberate cultivation.
I may not be presenting my thoughts in the most lucid
manner here, but clearly see that such cultivated geniuses
once existed in the world but never wrote anything like a
methodology on happiness. They did leave behind, though,
some mind-boggling cooking recipes, some bizarre stories
of spirits and angels, and a few compassionate yet paradoxical axioms. The legacy of Epicurus seems quite humble,
for he proposed "friendship, discourse and gourmet foods"
as the three ingredients of happiness. But this still doesn't
get to the semantic core of happiness. Can we find a specific instance that embodies "happiness" so that we can see
it with our own eyes? Yes, we can. We might ask: What does
"happiness" look like? Answer: It looks like a painting by
Cézanne. Happiness is painted one brushstroke at a time.
Cézanne himself, his wife, they were not happy....

The Boy Next Door

AS FOR CHILDHOOD PHOTOS, well, such photos will always become more precious as time passes. When you see someone's childhood photos next to those of his adulthood, you gradually discover that this child is indeed this youth, and indeed this middle-aged man and this elderly man. This process of intuitive identification is nothing short of magic, despite the rare exceptions when the person trying to process the identification is either inept or his own failing eyesight prevents him from doing so.

It is equally fascinating to look at the childhood photographs of your dearest love. You think to yourself: That was a different time, we were both children then, we didn't know each other, and how could I possibly know that I would later meet you, this exquisite you? Or perhaps the two of you became friends as children. Photos of both of you together then would be extraordinary. You'd say: Ah, yes, that was how things were, don't you remember? But I do.

A young man doesn't really know the value of his own

images as a child. It wasn't until I was in my forties that I retrieved my childhood photos and put them in a black, flat box together with the photos of my deceased parents. Sometimes I would open the box to pay respect to my parents, but I wouldn't linger over the image of my child-self for fear that memories of those gloomy days of bewilderment and painful loneliness would somehow resurface.

My sister was ten years older than me, and my *jiefu*, my sister's husband, was four years older than her. Eventually, as our other family members either died or disappeared, only my sister and Jiefu were around to mention how smart and vivacious I had been as a child, which to me sounded as if they were implying that I was now obtuse and indifferent. These retroactive applications of praise in no way tempered the bad memories of my childhood.

Who could have imagined that my photos would burn to ash in a catastrophic fire that would last more than ten years.

When the fire finally subsided, a friend of threw me a party in celebration of my survival. The party was held in her home as I didn't have a home anymore and she had built a new home to replace her old one that, like mine, had been destroyed. On her living room wall hung an enormous photograph of a child.

"Is that you?" I asked.

"Yes, when I was six."

"Very cute, looks exactly like you."

As soon as I said that a flood of unfortunate memories rushed over me. Trying to explain why I didn't possess a single childhood photo of myself was like an abandoned orphan trying to find an excuse for his parents.

After my sister died, the only living kin of my generation was my *jiefu*. He lived in a small town outside the city, and to visit him I had to take a ferry across the river and ride a bus another ten miles. His neighbor had a son named Weiliang. I would always stare in his direction with a vague, unexplainable feeling.

"Do you think Weiliang resembles anyone?" I finally asked Jiefu.

"Does he resemble anyone? Why, he looks just like you. I've wanted to tell you that for some time now. He looks exactly like you did as a child."

I was hoping my intuition would be confirmed but didn't think Jiefu would be so unequivocal.

"I guess there is a slight resemblance," I replied, "but I was an ugly duckling and Weiliang is very handsome."

He said with a big smile, "The resemblance is unmistakable. There's a noticeable physical likeness as well as a likeness of expression. Usually if someone looks at you, you don't stare directly into his eyes, though if the person doesn't look at you, you will turn to observe him."

"Doesn't everyone do that?"

"Not really ... besides, you look at people in a unique way, as does Weiliang."

After our conversation, I felt a slight trepidation whenever I saw the boy and would secretly hope that he wouldn't notice me so that I could observe him in silence. But the boy was acutely sensitive and would find ways to avoid me. If we did meet, he would blush and I would become speechless. But Jiefu continued to describe the subtle similarities he perceived between me and the boy. He doted on Weiliang and always praised him in front of me. I only listened with a smile. Wouldn't agreeing with him be the same as self-flattery?

Whenever I had some free time to cross the river and visit Jiefu, I couldn't help but think of the boy. What if I photographed him and asked Jiefu to select the few best ones to pass as if they were my own childhood photos? I felt a lightness thinking of this way to defy that catastrophic fire which had destroyed what should never have been destroyed. But my joy was soon overshadowed with worries: how could I convince Weiliang to change his hairstyle and clothes to correspond to the time period of my childhood?

The idea ebbed and flowed in my mind like the tide. Soon I simplified it to this: To ask Jiefu to take a photo with both Weiliang and me in it, which would be like juxtaposing my own images from two time periods. I could also claim without misgivings: This is me with my young friend Weiliang who looks like me as a child. But would Weiliang consent to the photograph? Children are naturally suspicious of adults.

A beautiful Sunday in spring arrived, and I realized I hadn't crossed the river for a while.

Nothing had changed in the small town, and nothing looked foreign. Jiefu had retired several years ago. We usually met in the city as he enjoyed the bustling pace of the place as he aged. We'd meet at a restaurant downtown for drinks so that he could revisit his old neighborhood and quench his nostalgic thirst. He had become very carefree about life and yet he was fastidious about certain details. When he moved, he drew me a map with directions of his new address, though of course I remembered every detail of his town.

Jiefu moved from the north part of town to the south. He lived in a new apartment complex. The place was so large and clean that it seemed almost dreary. He was so excited to see me that he bounced around awkwardly, repeating himself several times. I was touched by his childlike affection.

As we smoked, we compared his old neighborhood with his new one. I asked him, "Do you know if Weiliang and his family are still living in the same place?"

"Yes, they're still there."

"Do you see him at all?"

"Quite often. The boy enjoys chess and I'm giving him lessons."

"Now that's where he and I differ. I never liked chess as a child."

He laughed as if admitting a mistake. "How can the two of you be the same in everything!"

"Do you think I can see him today?"

"He'll come this afternoon. It's Sunday, isn't it? He always comes in the afternoon," he said. Then he added as if talking to himself, "I'll ask him to come."

I followed Jiefu out the door into the hallway. As he

gave a handful of candies to a little girl, asking her to be his messenger, I cautioned him, "Don't tell him. Don't let him know that I'm the one who wants to see him."

Jiefu turned around and said, "It's the same old you who knows all his whims."

The little messenger soon returned, giving her report while chewing a candy and leaning against the door frame. "Weiliang ... he's eating his lunch and says he'll come after the movie."

She waved a movie ticket in her hand and disappeared.

Jiefu insisted that we go to a restaurant where we could not only eat seasonal food, but also sit by the window so we could see the river and enjoy the willow branches dancing in the wind, smell the sweet aroma of rape flowers blowing across the water. After we were seated I told him about my secret wish that still ebbed and flowed like the tide.

"I think you've been thinking far too much," Jiefu said. "Taking photos isn't such a big deal. You can either take pictures of the boy or take pictures with the two of you together. Give a few to him and he'll be the one to say thank you."

"But it's not like photography in the usual sense of the word as I'm thinking of using his photos to replace mine that were burned. Perhaps I'd even use his photo in a book...."

Jiefu became silent, which shook my confidence. I considered abandoning my strange idea.

He lit a cigarette and began to speak slowly. "Your idea, I

believe, is neither right nor wrong. Weiliang only outwardly resembles your childhood self. In other respects he is entirely different. I ... I believe these childhood photos might be useful for you in the years ahead, but not to him...."

I smiled a helpless smile. "It is troubling. Am I being selfish, using his childhood like this? If so, I'd rather settle with the idea of being an orphan."

The light in his eyes dimmed, and then suddenly flashed. "No, no it isn't that. Let's do it this way. We should take the photos today and then find a first rate portrait artist to paint from the photos and change the style of dress to that of the 1930s. This will be you. Remember how much you liked that navy-blue soldier's shirt with big turned-over collars, and in cold weather you'd wear that traditional burgundy silk jacket, with a French hat tipped across your head?"

The old man glowed, wildly gesticulating.

"Here, please eat, eat.... All I want is the photograph of a child's face."

"This would be so easy to paint!"

"No ... no, I want a photograph not a painting. The image in a painting is a reflection of the painter. An artist who draws a portrait that doesn't reflect his inner being is a boring painter—I wouldn't like his work."

The food on the table was turning cold. We quickly ended our meal in case the little guest was already waiting for us.

Jiefu was, after all, much more experienced than I was. On the way back to his place, I accepted his suggestion:

We'd take the photos first and decide what to do with them later.

The little guest had not arrived yet. Jiefu cleaned the chessboard, then lit an incense stick, inserting it into a vase. Beyond the half-rolled bamboo blinds a ferry boat sounded its long horn.

When Weiliang arrived, my enthusiasm instantly vanished.

I realized that it had been three years since I had last seen him. Jiefu saw him frequently. He retained the impression of the boy three years before in his mind and didn't notice any changes since then.

The two of them became absorbed in a chess game while I watched intently. In his eyebrows, his nose, his forehead, Weiliang betrayed no resemblance to my childhood self. The dissimilarities as a whole constituted Weiliang—a good-looking youth in a village town who was completely different from me. His life would be more stable and fortunate.

Eighteen Passengers on a Bus

THERE WAS A TIME when our research institute owned two vehicles, a jeep and a minibus, and Li Shan was the only driver.

Li Shan was the institute's driver for three years. During his first two years he was cheerful and carefree, but sometime during his third year he became reticent. He would often be seen taking a nap in one of the vehicles. My coworkers hardly noticed the change in him. Since he had given me driving lessons, I approached him to see how he was doing. He told me that his married life wasn't harmonious. Not a rare thing, of course. People fall in love and get married, then life together relentlessly exposes each spouse's true nature to the other. If two rocks constantly rub against each other, each loses its rough edges—the man and woman henceforth live in uneventful mediocrity ("till death do we part" being the name of the drama). I put my hands on Li Shan's shoulder and consoled him: "Don't worry. Things will get better. Give it time. With time and patience, everything will be fine." He looked at me vaguely, which I took to be either an acknowledgment of gratitude or a sign of annoyance.

As I've gradually come to understand, *Hong Lou Meng* (*The Dream of the Red Mansion*) is a great novel not only because of its multi-layered meanings that have been widely commented on, but also because of this fascinating truth it reveals: any organization with one or two hundred employees interacting on a daily basis is similar to the kinship structure in *Hong Lou Meng*. Our institute was relatively small in size, with somewhere between one hundred and two hundred people. On the surface things seemed peaceful and prosperous, but in reality the workplace had disintegrated. Each resented the other and everyone blamed one another. This opaque, confusing, tension-filled atmosphere had been developing for a long time. Consequently, everyone had learned to play a specific role in the daily drama. Sometimes they hurt others to benefit themselves; sometimes they hurt others to no benefit at all. The pleasure derived from benefiting oneself wasn't always obtainable, but the pleasure derived from hurting others was easily obtainable at any time.

Whenever I breathed out a sigh of bitterness, my beloved would ask, "Why not find a different place to work?" And in turn I'd ask, "How is it now where you are?" And she'd reply, "The same, with fewer people." I'd then smile and say, "Well, you can transfer to my institute and I'll transfer to yours." I had in fact changed jobs five times and had experienced *Hong Lou Meng* five times. In the sixth chapter I assumed a supreme resignation.

One summer morning some colleagues and I were scheduled to attend a conference. A rowdy group of seventeen men sat in the company minibus, waiting for the driver. The passengers walked on and off, chatted noisily, snacked, made one last trip to the bathroom, until half an hour later they suddenly seemed to have settled their private business and discussions. Their attention turned to Li Shan: Where was he? He knew that he was supposed to drive us to the conference today, and even if he showed up now we'd be late.

There was still no sign of Li Shan.

I knew how to drive but didn't have a license. Plus part of the route was a curving mountainous road, and moreover I'd been through *Hong Lou Meng* five times already and wasn't about to volunteer to be the dumb Jiao Da character.

There was still no sign of Li Shan.

A few people got off the bus to try to find the Director or the Assistant Director, only to discover that one was on sick leave and the other was on a business trip. So they decided to return to their offices to make tea and smoke their cigarettes as if they had forgotten there was even a conference.

Li Shan finally appeared. Everyone stopped drinking tea and smoking cigarettes, boarded the bus, and began to bombard Li Shan with sarcasm and condemnation.

"Seventeen people have been waiting for you. Remember that you aren't the Director. Why should a driver act so superior as if he were our boss?"

"Look at the way he walks towards the bus, so very slowly, as if we deserved it. Hey, Li Shan, don't you know what you do for a living!"

"We might as well pay you a fee plus tips. Just tell us how much for each person, Li Shan. If you were on strike, why did you come? You don't have to work today. It could make a difference if you lasted two weeks."

"You must have forgotten and thought it was your wedding night. Getting out of bed this morning wasn't easy considering how you had to struggle to part with her."

"Or perhaps your wife was going through a difficult labor last night. I assume you had to wait until the baby was born before leaving home and rushing over here."

"My guess is that your wife eloped with someone. Quick, start the car and drive 200 kilometers per hour. We'll help you catch that wife of yours, together with her lover."

Li Shan didn't say a word. Ever since I had started taking driving lessons from him, it had become routine that I'd sit in the front seat. These glib-tongued cracks angered me so much that I shouted, "We all have our own problems! So he's late once, one rare occurrence! Don't you people have any shame, talking the way you do?"

"Rare occurrence, indeed, he's such a rare talent. So it's our fault that we don't know how to drive. But a certain person here does know how to drive but doesn't help Li Shan. He thinks he's the good guy here."

Their vicious discourse now attacked me. This was how they usually talked during bus trips, out of boredom. Each of them had at one time or another asked Li Shan for help. Whether they needed help moving, or to transport something, or to attend a wedding or funeral, or to take a random excursion—they had each privately asked Li Shan to be their driver. A year before, this carefree young man had been willing to take a risk or violate the rules to help them, to graciously serve these people. But for the past year he had been ignoring their requests. And they remembered only their recent grievances, not the previous favors. They figured that an opportunity to mount sarcastic attacks presented itself that day. After all, Li Shan was now quite useless to them; he was only worth mocking and discarding.

"Seriously, she has a pretty face and a shapely figure. Li Shan, you have exquisite taste in women and you're a very lucky guy. You should have asked your wife to wait for us by the road. I could have grabbed her waist to rescue her, whisk her onto the bus. Hey, it's summer and the little clothes she'd be wearing would make the honeymoon much easier."

"What honeymoon? They've been married for over a year and are no longer newly weds."

"I'm talking about myself going on a honeymoon with his wife. Of course it's the husband's obligation to be the driver."

Laughter roared in the bus.

"Ah, women, women are vehicles and men are the driv-
ers. I think Li Shan can drive vehicles of metal, but not vehicles of flesh."

"As for his bus, the windows have long been broken and
the doors forced open."

The bus erupted in more laughter.

Sixteen males spoke in turn as if they were at a conference. Each of them saw a chance to display his own wit.
I glanced over at Li Shan who looked calm, revealing an
enormous threshold for tolerance.

"Shut up, all of you. No talking to the driver. Why don't
you all talk about your own families, about being saints to
your own chaste virgins. What goes on in the Li family is
none of your business."

The bus lurched forward and slowed to a squeaking stop.
Li Shan turned to me wide-eyed and said in a threatening
tone, "What is it to you if anything happens in my family?"

I was stunned. "What is it to me ... what ...?"

"Let them talk their talk. No need for you to be so wordy."

He leaped out of the bus, crossed over to my side in a
few swift steps, opened the door, and pulled me out.

"And you blame me?!" I asked, outraged.

Li Shan jumped back into the driver's seat and slammed
the door shut. I held onto the edge of the open window. He
released the brake, and as he stepped on the gas he raised his
fist and leaned over to knock me loose, giving me a vigor-
ous punch. I fell onto my back and saw the vehicle tilt for
a brief moment and then speed forward.

"Li Shan! ... Li Shan! ..." I shouted helplessly.

The bus shot ahead like an arrow—I watched it careen off the highway, float in the air for a second, and plummet into the deep valley below. A loud explosion followed and birds flew into the air in every direction.

I was horror-struck.

An empty feeling washed over me; blinding sunlight reflected off the surface of the road.

It was only after a long, long while that I heard the birds chirping and the wind rustling the trees.

I stumbled to the cliff and saw only the deep valley below, covered in vegetation. There was no trace of the bus, no trace of the passengers. There was nothing....

Those sixteen passengers certainly didn't deserve to die. I decided to find out why Li Shan was late. All I could learn was that his wife had upset him. It wasn't one or two things, but an accumulation of many things. Nobody could clarify further—only Li Shan himself knew what had happened.

Quiet Afternoon Tea

BEFORE I MOVED HERE, no young person had set foot in this house for a very long time. Since my arrival, my aunt, the sister of my father, has been warning me that I should choose my social circle with discretion. I have no problems with that, even if this isn't a convent. Eventually, I'll return to the world of the young, and the house will become part of the world of the young.

Visitors in general are rare, and the old couple doesn't go out much. From what I can tell, those who once frequently called on friends cannot be bothered to do so when they are old, and even avoid such visits to conserve energy.

I believe my aunt and uncle weren't so withdrawn in their youth. When the occasional visitor drops by, I over-hear them speak about who has moved, who has been suc-cessful, who is suffering from a strange illness, who is still doing what before death ... details, distinctly remembered, mingle in the cross sections of the distant past. It is said that the older one grows the further one's memory reaches into the deep past. I've also noticed a common mistake the visitors, men or women, invariably make: all of them compliment the host, remarking how he doesn't look his age and how he retains his youthful appearance, while they really should offer this sort of bouquet to the hostess. Or they should say something like, "Neither of you looks your age" or "Both of you have retained your youthful appearance."

Aunt is thus jealous of her husband, often casting a cold glance at him as if sizing up a stranger, as if she were calculating how much substance the compliment contained and how much was meant to flatter.

Uncle is quite content with himself. Those compliments have convinced him that refusing to look old is his natural obligation. He is so meticulously neat and tidy that he will not relax his appearance even at home. He has fine taste in ties, and he wears sock garters. But his greatest advantage is that he doesn't gain weight anymore. Though he wears a belt, his old clothes still fit. In my eyes, however, he's still a conservative old gentleman who shows many signs of decay. Those visitors his age are crotchety ancients, mocking themselves, admitting they've seen better days. Mere children during World War II, they are serious about everything, much more serious than our generation.

Although Aunt supposedly started dieting five years ago, her weight hasn't changed. She seems to be suspended in her rotund state, and it is unlikely she will ever be slim. But as her shape is more or less fixed, she continues the ritual of afternoon tea and biscuits once or twice a month.

"I suppose someone is coming for a visit today?" Aunt asks.

"I doubt anyone is," says Uncle.

"Are you not going out?"

"Where to? I am going nowhere," he says. "Would you like to go somewhere for fun?"

"The weather isn't so good … But I wouldn't want to even if the weather were good."

"We haven't done anything outdoors for a long time," he says, trying to improve her reasoning.

"I always feel depressed when we return," she sighs.

"So do I," he echoes.

"That is a nice tie. Is it new?"

"The narrower type is in fashion. I don't know when I bought this one. Too wide. It's better not to wear it often. It doesn't match my shirt."

"Wasn't the narrow type in fashion some time ago?"

"Toward the end of the '50s, yes." With his thumb and index finger he draws the shape of a narrow tie on his chest.

Aunt is just as devoted to her appearance. Sometimes she asks me, "What is the latest fashion, Alice? I don't have time to go shopping. Can't you help me find a few things from my closet that bears some resemblance to current trends?"

I admire her thinking, for fashion is nothing but a cycle of renewing the old. Advertisers and designers are quite shrewd. Every time they create a new trend, they make a few additions and deletions so the old, in its new form, seems unfamiliar. That's why I feel sorry for Aunt. Luckily, she only tries to catch up with the latest fashion at home, which spares her public embarrassment. So I always choose a few things that look similar to new designs. This pleases her. She looks at herself in the mirror and smiles, saying, "Are you certain this is popular again? It was fashionable a long time ago, when I was in my forties."

She is flattered by her own foresight and by the fact that she can still fit, albeit with some difficulty, into her old clothes. Evidently, she has been quite plump for much of her life.

Aunt continues to sit in the living room, her back straight. Her fashionable clothes enhance her energy. She still waits for her husband to acknowledge the hint in her words. "A narrower tie makes one feel more sprightly than the wider type, doesn't it?"

"Perhaps you're right."

"And if you simply do without a tie?"

Uncle feels the sting of her words and says in his own defense, "I'm accustomed to it and wouldn't feel as comfortable with the collar loose."

She accepts his compromise. "That's true. Take sleeves. I don't like when people roll up the long sleeves of their shirt. Why not simply wear short sleeves then? It doesn't look nice with long sleeves rolled up."

"That's indeed more proper. Such people have no sense of ... *grammar.*"

So Uncle will continue to wear his ties and be grammatical.

Aunt turns to me. "How long has it been since we last had tea?"

"About ten days."

"How about today, then?"

"Sure, I'll see to it. What do you think, Uncle?"

"Fine with me."

The occasional afternoon tea doesn't require much preparation. The whole ritual is essentially for looking at fine china and silverware adorned with a little sugar, a few biscuits, a little jam, and milk. It isn't the preparation that makes me feel dread. It's the anticipation that I'll again be subjected to Aunt's well-rehearsed story.

According to custom, I do not arrange the tea set on the table before I invite the masters of the house to take their seats. They must be seated face to face at the table in expectation for me to bring out the tea set on a tray and place each item not only in the right spot but in the right sequence. When tea is served, I have to ask, with fake innocence, "Would anyone care for some butter?"

Aunt then shakes her head and Uncle is silent.

"What about a tiny bit of cheese?"

"No, thank you. But I wouldn't mind if you have some."

This is sufficient indication that Aunt is in a good mood. She usually desires nothing more than the sound of "butter" and "cheese." In this way she is able to express slight mourning so that her mild sadness can be a lot sweeter. Although I will inherit their house in the future, my present role is that of servant and companion. Before, after I just moved in, I was in a constant state of anxiety. As time passed, things became easier to deal with, though neither of them has made a will yet.

Afternoon tea is almost over. After a silent pause, the casual atmosphere of sipping tea and chewing biscuits begins to fade into space. In the darkening twilight, Aunt's voice rises: "That day, I remember it was October 26th, the air-raid siren started at one o'clock in the afternoon, and the all-clear was heard at three. You came home at seven o'clock. Minus the hour on the road, there were three unaccountable hours. Where were you during that period of time?"

Uncle doesn't flinch.

It's customary that on Aunt's face there's an expression of confidence that she'll receive an answer, and on Uncle's face the indication of determination that he won't reply. Twilight is darkening. After afternoon tea and such conversational reverberations, one becomes aware of how the twilight darkens or, rather, how it thickens to the point of being stagnant. Aunt is still; Uncle is still; and I, too, am still.

Only as Aunt stretches herself does Uncle adjust his position slightly and I begin to move my limbs. It's an old rule of the house that the master doesn't turn on or off the light in the living room. Instead she shouts, "Alice! Turn on the light, please!" or "You can turn off the light in the living room now, Alice!"

While I wait for the order, twilight fades into night. The tips of their silhouetted noses vaguely glisten. Their expressions are already invisible.

"The 26th, it was October the 26th that day. The afternoon air-raid siren started at one o'clock and the all-clear was announced around three o'clock. Your trip home would take no more than an hour. But when you came home it was already seven o'clock. Where were you during the other three hours?"

Silence.

It's now completely dark in the living room. The silver doesn't shine anymore.

"Alice, remove the tea set."

I feel pardoned and hasten to the kitchen to clean up. The clinking of cups and saucers is music to my ears. I cherish these antiques and often feel pleasantly moved by their delicate refinement.

"Alice, are you finished? You can turn on the light now."

I dry my hands and turn on the light—everything's the same as it was before. This is merely a dream.

Another day. The three of us watch the gardener mow the lawn; we enjoy the fragrant smell of fresh-cut grass. But Aunt soon finds the smell too strong and starts to itch. She goes inside to take a bath.

I take the chance to whisper in Uncle's ear, "What day was that?"

"What day was what?"

"The air-raid siren."

"Oh, that was World War II, forty, fifty years ago."

"You were just married then."

"Just married. Every other day or two days the air-raid siren would blare. But it didn't necessarily mean there would be bombing."

"When it was clear, where did you go?"

"Nowhere."

"During those three hours?"

"Ah … it was like this. When there was a siren and the all-clear wasn't heard until after three o'clock, you didn't have to work for the rest of the day. Some people would wait for the sound of the siren and once inside the shelter keep looking at their watches for fear that there would be an all-clear before three."

"But you came home at seven?"

"I always came home immediately after work—that was the case every day. If there was an air-raid siren and I didn't have to work for the rest of the day, I'd go home directly."

"What about October 26th, between four and seven?"

"I was home."

"But Aunt said you didn't go home until seven?"

"I was home by four."

"How can that be?"

"It cannot be clearer. I came out of the shelter and looked at my watch. A few minutes to three. Of course it meant I didn't have to work. So I took a bus and came home earlier than usual. The wooden fence in the backyard was broken and I went to assess what repairs were needed …"

"You did the repair?"

"No, I had to hire someone."

"What happened next?"

"I put my briefcase in the study and went to the living room. No one was there. I walked upstairs and didn't find your Aunt in the bedrooms either. The doors to the kitchen and the bathroom were open. The door to the basement was closed. So I assumed that she wasn't home."

"Did she go somewhere?"

"Where could she have gone? She had mentioned that she wanted to learn how to make pickled cucumbers from our neighbor behind our house. So I went next door and Miss Toby said she had indeed come, but that was at noon the day before. Miss Toby also said that Mr. James's dog Hairy had some puppies and maybe she had gone to see them. I thought that was unlikely ..."

"So Aunt was at home?"

"But she wasn't. Mr. James invited me in to see the puppies. I thought the puppies were dirty but didn't say so. I only said that we didn't know how to raise animals. Mr. James suggested that we go fishing and he showed me his fishing set. I said that I didn't smoke a pipe. He said that had nothing to do with fishing. I said that the fish wouldn't bite so easily and it would take too long to catch anything. He replied that waiting was the interesting part ..."

"Where did you go next?" I asked, deliberately cutting him off.

"I didn't go anywhere. I looked at Mr. James's collection of plant samples. There were even some beautiful imitation plants made of glass that looked nearly the same as the real ones. He also had a butterfly collection. There were several varieties that I had never seen before, incredibly beautiful ..."

"What next?"

"I went back home."

"About what time?"

"About ... not sure. I didn't look at my watch as it was getting dark."

"Where was Aunt?"

"She was sitting against a pillar on the front porch. Her hands were cold."

"She questioned you, I assume?"

"She said, 'So you are back then?' and I said, 'Yes, I'm back.'"

"What next?"

"Nothing."

"How can you say nothing?"

"Because nothing else was said."

"Why, then, did she ask you again, just a few days ago?"

"Of course it wasn't the first time you heard that. For forty years she's asked every now and then."

"Why don't you explain?"

"In the beginning, I thought why ask about such a simple thing and why answer it, so I said nothing. I thought if I didn't say anything she would stop asking. Later, as she asked more frequently, I thought if I answered she wouldn't believe me. She would say: 'If it was really nothing, why didn't you say that before?' How can I respond to that?"

"And you never asked why she wasn't home that day?"

"No. I suspect she must have been waiting on the front porch by four o'clock. I didn't know because I entered from the backyard. I guess this is what happened."

"Now what?"

"Now?"

"I mean if she asks you again, are you going to answer her?"

"I cannot explain myself clearly now."

"Don't you feel uncomfortable during afternoon tea?"

"Oh, yes, very uncomfortable."

"If you explained yourself, you wouldn't feel so tortured."

"It's too late. I can never clear it up."

"But you told me just now as if it had happened yesterday. You have a very good memory. You don't have to wait till she asks. Simply go to her and explain."

"She won't believe me. She will never believe me. She'll think that I've been concocting this tale for many years. As for Miss Toby and Mr. James, one is dead and the other moved to Canada. Maybe he, too, is dead. Even if he is still alive, who can remember what happened between four and seven o'clock forty-some years ago on October 26th?"

"That doesn't matter. You don't need a witness. Let the truth out and you won't have to suffer anymore!"

"Even as an observer you must have felt tortured?"

"Yes, me too."

The gardener is gone, leaving behind a flat carpet of a lawn. It suddenly occurs to me that Aunt might suspect Uncle and me of talking about her behind her back. So I quickly enter the house. Aunt usually needs a nap after a bath. I tiptoe back downstairs.

"How is she?" Uncle asks.

"Asleep. It'd be better if you find an opportunity to tell her tomorrow."

The next day nobody mentions afternoon tea. If either Uncle or I proposed it, it would have seemed like a conspiracy, making it even more difficult to convince Aunt. She might even suspect that Uncle and I had planned to entrap her. That would put my status and future at risk.

Without urging Uncle on, I let things take their own course. I even try not to talk to Uncle when Aunt isn't present.

Two weeks later: a clear day after a rain. Birds chirp all morning into the afternoon.

"What a fine day!" I say, stretching myself.

Uncle glances my way.

Aunt looks out the window. "Alice, it has been quite some time since we had our afternoon tea, has it not?"

"I bought some Dutch biscuits a few days ago."

"It's still early. We shall have our tea in a little while. Tea, of course, not coffee."

When I turn around, I see Uncle's back as he walks out of the living room.

I walk outside onto the porch and bask in the sunshine, deep in thought.

Of the three of us, I must be the only one who feels excited. Aunt doesn't know that her husband is going to prove his complete fidelity and innocence. Uncle has to prepare his defense and must be nervous. I only pray that there'll be no complications with my role here; nobody knows for certain when the servant will become the master. They are old and I'm not getting any younger. If no other legal heir suddenly emerges, my status seems secure. I'll raise my dogs and cats and make my own pickled cucumbers. Oh, Lord, forgive me for thinking these thoughts. I pray for Uncle and Aunt, wishing them health and long life. I don't have any money right now. If I did, I would ask the priest to hold a mass for my benefactors ...

"Alice, are you making the preparations?"

"What time is it?" I ask, even though I'm wearing my watch.

"Four o'clock."

"I'll start making the tea."

It could be a coincidence: Aunt looks particularly well; Uncle's thin hair is neatly combed. I could've changed into another dress, but am afraid that Aunt will make some connection in retrospect and suspect that I had learned earlier than she did what she should have known long ago. Her serious concern for forty years has no significance to me whatsoever.

The silver is polished to a shine and the china looks sparkling new. I haven't broken anything in the three years I've lived here. I urge Uncle to prove his innocence so that: first, Aunt can finally feel relieved that her husband hasn't failed her in any of his deeds; second, Uncle can free himself from this embarrassing situation—the resolution of a forty-year-old suspicion can at last clear his name as a perfect gentleman; and third, I'm reaching my limit having to bear the oppressive silence. Aunt should face her husband alone in dealing with their past. Obviously she's wanted a third party to play witness, though I really cannot play this supporting role any longer. Please no more of this unfortunate supporting role.

Aunt and Uncle, as usual, are sitting across from one another in the middle of oval table. I sit at the lower end; the seat at the upper end is vacant. I've pushed the flower vase aside so that there's more room for the tea set. Suddenly, I become worried that Aunt won't ask the question today or ever again. Would this be good or bad? If she doesn't ask, we'll be spared the torture, but the forty-year-old suspicion will never be resolved. So it would be better if she asks today. If she asks another time, Uncle, as usual, will not move nor speak, as if a chair sitting in another chair.

It's still bright outside, night still far away. If it rains, it will get dark sooner, and the sound of the rain will make Aunt feel agitated.

What if Uncle doesn't reply? And feels that his pride would be too injured to explain something that doesn't need explaining? Shall I then speak on his behalf? Could I? Aunt would ask: Why should you speak for him?

"You are right. They are good," Aunt says, chewing a biscuit.

"Right about what?" asks Uncle.

I quickly return from my thoughts and pick up a biscuit.

"That these biscuits are better than those made in Denmark."

"You don't say. Let me try one." Uncle reaches for one as Aunt pushes the plate toward him.

"Today's tea is good, too!" Aunt praises.

"Do you know how I made it?"

"I don't know, but it has such a nice aroma!"

"It reminds me of a landscape in spring!" Uncle rubs his hands before picking up his cup again.

"Spring may come again, but the spring of life will never return!"

Old people talking about spring is no different from old people singing. I must stop that singing. "Well," I explain, "it was a schoolmate, a Chinese man, who taught me. They call it *hong-cha*, 'red tea.' You boil the red tea leaves then add dried rose petals, making sure that the lid is covered tight to keep the aroma in. As for what they call *lü-cha*, 'green tea,' you pour boiling water directly onto the leaves. The heat should be turned off when the water just begins to simmer. Jasmine can be added. I guess the principle is not unlike matching red wine with meat and chilled white wine with fish …"

"Exactly, it is about matching—harmony!"

"Indeed, it is the same for people," says Aunt.

I stand up to refill their cups.

"Your schoolmate, that Chinese man, what happened to him?"

"He went back home."

"Did you often have tea together?"

"We were in college."

"He was meticulous in what he did, was he not?" Aunt says, watching me.

"So it seemed."

"He must be meticulous, and that is why you still remember him."

"I only remember that you add rose petals to the red tea."

"Rose—the Chinese may not even know what roses really are."

Aunt looks tempted to sing again. I have to change the subject quickly. "Aunt, do you think we'd better buy some more of these biscuits?"

"Nothing tastes as good as before the war. Biscuits and fruits have become more and more tasteless!"

"Perhaps it is our taste buds that are fading," says Uncle.

"I refuse to believe that!"

"Actually, I think it's mainly the quality of the wheat and flour," says Uncle.

"Yes, chemical fertilizers and growth hormones may increase production, but the natural qualities of cereals and fruits are compromised." I have to say something to agree with him.

"Even flowers don't smell sweet anymore. Oh, the flower sellers in those days. A couple of flower sellers in the street and the entire neighborhood is filled with sweet smells."

Outside the window it was turning dusk, the living room slowly darkening. Time to hold my tongue. Uncle, I see, is gently rubbing his hands.

Aunt raises her cup and then puts it down. A silver spoon

turns around in a saucer.

"That day, I remember it was October 26th, the air-raid siren began at one o'clock in the afternoon and the all-clear was heard at three. You came home at seven o'clock. Minus the hour on the road, there were three unaccountable hours. Where had you been ..."

Uncle stops rubbing his hands. Silence.

I cough softly, covering my mouth.

Silence lengthens and lengthens visibly. I have to occupy myself by pouring them more tea. The spout of the teapot bumps the edge of their cups. I mutter an apology.

"October 26th, 1944. The siren sounded at one in the afternoon and the all-clear was heard close to three. It would take no more than an hour on the road. It was after seven when you came home. Where had you been during those three hours ..."

Uncle.

I turn my wristwatch around to see what time it is but cannot see clearly.

Perhaps Uncle prefers my absence. I leave them to go to the bathroom.

I stand in the darkness of the bathroom, leaving the door ajar.

There isn't a sound.

I look at my watch up close and see that it's 6:55.

Then it's seven o'clock. I wash my hands and return to the living room.

"Alice, please turn on the light."

Fellow Passengers

IT WAS LIGHTLY RAINING one early morning in autumn.
A few people waited at a remote bus stop in a suburb of
Shanghai.

I boarded the bus and picked a seat near the window.
Outside the window right below me a man and woman
were saying their good-byes.

Woman: "It's time to board the bus. We'll never finish
this conversation."

Man: "My sister isn't evil incarnate. She does have good
intentions at times."

Woman: "Good intentions? She has good intentions, indeed." The woman slashed her hand slowly across her neck
and added, "I wouldn't believe that if you killed me."

Man, after a pause: "Tempers flare easily, you know. My
sick mother isn't going to get better. Forgive her."

Woman: "Sick? I'm sick, too. You mother and sister together are capable of all sorts of tricks."

Man: "That's why I'm always afraid to come home.... "

Woman: "I wouldn't care if you didn't come home again. They already laugh at me as if I were a widow."

Man: "Now that's obscene."

The city was separated from the suburbs by a river. Many who worked in the city only went home on weekends. Most of these commuters were cheerful. I suspected that the man and woman were newlyweds. The woman couldn't bear to part from her husband so she rose early to see him off in the rain. From their brief conversation it was apparent that the woman didn't get along with her in-laws. The man obviously couldn't do much about it. Even though they were newlyweds, even though their periods of separation must have brought them even closer to each other, they had more worries than happiness. That she and her mother-in-law and sister-in-law had to live under the same roof was the main cause of their sad domestic situation. In the confines of their home, they couldn't avoid each other and could barely live with each other. I could tell from their pale and weary faces that they hadn't slept well the night before. When the husband came home, the woman's complaints of the past week would naturally pour out of her, her voice rising to a fervent pitch. His mother and sister would also complain to him and would make a list of his wife's wrongdoings, perhaps even delving into trifling details. Why couldn't they live in separate homes? Perhaps there was a housing shortage or perhaps they didn't have the money to rent another place. Complicated affairs often have simple explanations.

I was content with my leisure and private insights. And I considered myself experienced in reading humans. Besides, with no family, my life was much simpler than a god's.

The bus was about to leave. The couple exchanged a long glance. Then the man jumped onto the bus and sat in the seat in front of me. The woman passed the black umbrella to him from an open window and ran into the rain, head down.

The man hung up his umbrella. He sat still for a moment and then bent forward, weeping into the back of the seat in front of him.

A fellow passenger in tears would otherwise have little to do with me. But by chance I had overheard their conversation, had seen their pale faces, and had even speculated about their situation. The other passengers were probably unaware of his troubles.

Being selfish and often particular about people's appearances, I usually wasn't particularly inclined to compassion. If the weak and the victimized seemed ugly to me, they could hardly arouse my pity. I was often conscious of my lack of generosity and chastised myself for superficially judging people. But then I also forgave myself for the same reason because what I saw as ugly sometimes actually reflected the heart of the person.

The weeping man didn't evoke any ugliness. He was dressed plainly and had handsome features, including proportionately thick eyebrows. He was of medium stature, perhaps not quite thirty years old. I could see how his slender shoulders spasmodically heaved beneath his navy blue jacket; I could hear how he expressed his suffering nasally and how he let out intermittent long sighs while shaking his head.... I felt an urge to stroke his back and talk to him about the possibility of a more harmonious relationship between his mother, sister, and his wife.... I wanted to tell him that everything would be fine, just fine.

I realized I first needed to close the window. It wasn't summer anymore and the man was thinly clothed.

As his sobs lessened, my thoughts of conversing with him also faded. Some people weep in a hidden place hoping to be discovered. Others weep in a hidden place where they don't wish to be found. These two mindsets could characterize the same person, possibly different expressions under different circumstances.

The book in my satchel could stop these aimless thoughts.

He must have fallen asleep. He looked so fragile I was afraid he might catch a cold. I wanted to take off my jacket and cover his shoulders but I hesitated for fear of waking him up. I wasn't sure why I felt so eager to help him, while also feeling afraid of being too friendly ... But should I watch him while he caught a cold ... I could wake him up but then he would weep again ... Well, let him sleep then ... since his wedding day all his weekends have been consumed with family conflicts ... He probably had never anticipated such problems before marrying ... or perhaps he had but decided to get married anyway ...

It seemed as if I were holding a kind of dialogue with him.

I returned to my book.

The bus neared its destination. I put my book away. Just as I was about to wake the man up, he was wakened by a sudden jerk of the bus and raised his head—then remembered his umbrella. I saw his face again when we got off: he indeed had been sleeping.

The surface of the road glimmered in the sunlight. The man walked ahead of me toward the ferry, his gait slightly wavering. Suddenly he started twirling his umbrella, making circles and circles—clockwise, counter-clockwise— while he whistled to the rhythm of the twirling.

It was the same man with a navy blue jacket and black umbrella.

The ferryboat was crowded with passengers. I stood at the bow, facing the wind. I had often thought that a human being is like a container holding both joy and sadness. But a human being isn't a container. He is more like a pipe through which both joy and sadness flow. A pipe with all sorts of emotions flowing through it until one's death or until it is emptied. A madman, then, is someone whose pipe is stuffed, or cracked....

He who can feel sadness easily can feel cheerfulness more easily. Thus he possesses a strong capacity for survival. He whose pipe thickens must be slow in feeling either joy or sadness. A blocked pipe eventually breaks. The world is made up of many unblocked pipes like the man in navy blue with his black umbrella. I should be able to twirl my umbrella in his lighthearted manner after I have wept and grieved. Or else I should always be excluded from the world which includes them. They are insignificant people. I am less than insignificant.

Weimar in Early Spring

IN THE TEMPERATE ZONE, at the start of each season, a
sacred aura delicately begins to insinuate itself in the wind.
While winter lingers on, spring's cold air feels tender and
moist as it stirs up private, fleeting memories. Each passing
day silently acknowledges the change of seasons so that the
beginning of spring is received with paramount propriety
and somberness. If it should turn clear and warm in an in-
stant, if the birds should suddenly fly and chirp without re-
straint, the weather would just as quickly, as if from remorse,
turn gloomy, and might even result in freezing sleet.

Spring doesn't arrive so easily. Spring is like a melan-
choly yet dignified man. It is no wonder then that a person with deep addictions is sometimes likened to spring.
Toward the end of March, in this temperate region, humidity from the earth's interior rises and spreads across the
plains by the sea. A hazy fog fills the early morning but by

noon the fog transforms into huge clouds that seem suspended by the sunlight in the air. When dusk falls, the horizon starts to blur, and the more it blurs, the closer its desire moves toward you. Borders in the fields become unrecognizable while cottages, churches, and wetlands in the woods are immersed in a milky mist. Night doesn't seem to turn dark on time. Eventually, a full moon hangs in the heavens, a pool of yellowish haze, solemn and vast in design, not unlike a refined maze.

Although spring may resemble a man with deep addictions, the man may not know that he shares this likeness with it. When a cold current comes, the wind is so strong that the windows and doors of a house have to be shut tight. Inside, there is a table covered with a thick layer of dust and a fire burning in the hearth as in a storybook. The delicate sacred aura has vanished. Look at the willows, the camellias, the magnolia lilies, the devilwood jasminum nudiflorum. They tell you that spring continues its progress. If one day, in the distance, you see a row of willows appear ghostly, as if the fog was saturated with particles of green powder, then spring is finally here. The willow branches heavy with tender buds seem coquettish yet openhearted and make one wonder if this isn't a seductively charming woman. But of course spring is no person.

I imagine a mythology of flowers, flowers created during a grand competition among the gods. One god invented the lily, another god the tulip. Here appeared peonies and there water lilies. As soon as the colorful flowers of morning were completed, they turned to the evening hues. Each god worked incessantly, creating one type of flower after another. Or perhaps the gods were grouped in kinds and kinships, creating their own categories of flowers. It was clear which flowers were the favorite works of which gods, which were rough drafts or revised versions, which were collages made with extraneous materials, and which were simply extraneous materials dumped upon leaves and grass. One can see that the divine competition was held in haste and that the gods had no previous experience in creating flowers.

Take the rose family for example. The gods began with the multiflora and when they found it too plain, tried the aeieularis. But the aeieularis seemed a bit too complex so they switched to the indica; this, they felt, still lacked a certain elegance so finally they created their masterpiece, the rose rugose. Thus the briars, the rosebushes, the China roses, and roses of all other varieties came into being, whether they were woody or herbaceous, unifoliate or multifoliate. Roses are dicotyledons, lined with leaves, the flowers invariably possessing five petals and sepals. Stamens are even more numerous, and the superior or inferior position of the ovary occurred at a later stage in the flower's evolution. Whether the fruits should be capsules or berries was the work of another god.

By the time this grand competition finally ended, all the gods were exhausted. They also had become weak-willed and had grown so attached to their playthings that they inserted their genetic code into their works of art. Who should be the one formulating the codes? I imagine it was the most levelheaded of all the gods. Perhaps he had thus far remained a passive observer of the competition. The other gods were worn out but the unsatisfactory drafts, the collages, the extraneous materials had not been destroyed. The levelheaded god scattered genetic code over the flowers like raindrops. Afterward, the gods all flew away, laughing into the firmament. A rainbow appeared in the sky. Flowers on the earth bloomed for a long time without wilting because they were the first generation of flowers.

The science of botany that emerged much later is entirely unable to account for the diversity of flowers, but the botanist, with some grumblings, can nonetheless make distinctions between the concealed and revealed, between the angiospermous and gymnospermous.

No need to elaborate on the obvious beauty and splendor of flowers. Simply consider how the petals and pistils and sepals and stems and stalks and leaves all coexist with such harmony in each and every type of flower. Are the flowers themselves aware of this design? Is it possible that the beasts, birds, reptiles, and insects might be aware of this harmony? Plants can reproduce themselves via the spore, kernel, and roots. But how flowers and leaves can survive through such efficient means is astounding. As for the cryptogamia (seedless plants), are ferns, lichens, fungi, algae, and figs not found everywhere and anywhere? Do flowers display their divine beauty for their own enjoyment and pleasure? Not likely. The authors of flowers have bestowed their own sights and scents onto human beings. Or perhaps the gods first made flowers and then proceeded to make humans who could appreciate the flowers.

There is this tree the fortunate have witnessed.

One winter, after a number of warm days, thick clouds gathered in the sky. Tens of thousands of crows flew out of the woods and hovered in circles. The villagers named this phenomenon "the yelling for snow" and the gathering of thick clouds "the brewing of snow." In the freezing wind, a traveler on his way home noticed light purple buds on the strong boughs of a tree growing vigorously. The branches were heavy with abundant buds. Snowflakes began to dance in the sky and the buds bloomed into flowers as if this were an arranged rendezvous with the snow. The heavier the snowfall grew, the bigger the blooming flowers expanded. The tree stood about ten meters tall with a trunk around one and half meters wide; its leaves resembled camphor or poplar foliage, its crown wide and full. The flowers were white as snow like Japanese cherry blossoms and released a delicate aroma. That winter there were several snowfalls and the tree bloomed several times accordingly. When a snow flurry first began, the tree showed no sign of change and remained still. But as the snow thickened and blanketed the land, one could smell the tree's sweet aroma spreading intensely through the day and into the night. As soon as the snow stopped, the blooming also ended.

There is no scientific name recorded for this particular tree. But the tree indeed exists, south of China's Dongting Lake near the Shuikou Mountains in Dongkou County, Hunan Province. It's been there for at least two hundred years.

When winter ended in 1832, spring still brought spells of freezing cold.

On March 15th, Goethe stepped out for a walk and caught a cold. He recovered quickly though and was soon out of bed, walking in small steps while longing for spring warmth.

But on the evening of March 20th his health took a sudden turn for the worse. He decided not to see a doctor immediately.

On March 21st, Goethe either rested in bed or sat in an armchair next to his bed. He seemed frightened and ill at ease. Dr. Fugel arrived and eased his suffering somewhat, but he had already lost all his strength. At 11:30 on March 22nd, Goethe died. It was a Thursday.

Friday morning, Frederick opened the bedroom door and entered. Goethe lay on his back, in eternal peace. It seemed as if there were still thoughts flowing behind his wide forehead. His face showed a calm resolve. Frederick wanted to take a lock of his hair as a keepsake but then felt uneasy as he was cutting it. Goethe's naked body was covered with a white sheet and surrounded by huge blocks of ice. Frederick gently lifted the white sheet with both of his hands and saw that Goethe's chest was firm and broad, his arms and legs muscular and not just bones, his two feet small and distinctly shaped. There was no flabby flesh on his entire body. Around his heart was absolute silence.

While on his deathbed, Goethe had asked what date it was, and then said, "So, spring has begun—I'll recover even faster."

Eight years before, when spring approached on the cusp of its arrival, Goethe, in his perfectly elegant manner, welcomed Heinrich Heine to his home. They conversed about the sacred aura that suffuses each season, about the divine competition among the gods, and about a tree south of Dongting Lake. They also spoke of the trees along the road between Jena and Weimar, how the poplar trees had not yet grown leaves, and how enchanting the scenery would be during a midsummer sunset.

Goethe suddenly asked, "What are you writing right now?"

Heine replied, "Faust."

At the time, part two of Goethe's *Faust* had not yet been published.

"Mr. Heine, I assume that you still have other business to attend to in Weimar."

"The moment I stepped into your home, dear sir, all of my business in Weimar was completed."

As soon as Heine said that, he stood up and bowed to take leave.

Such mannered behavior was quite characteristic of Goethe as it was equally characteristic of Heine.

Even tonight, a night filled with the same freezing air of spring, I'm still tormented by the desire to write the story of Faust. After all, the ink in which Faust signed his contract with Mephistopheles is not yet dry. And though it's true Gretchen performs certain deeds, neither Helen nor Euphorion had any active roles assigned to them in the drama. The ending also seems predictable: Faust falls and is rescued. Nonetheless, when things occur and end in mythology, epic, or tragedy, they just occur and end. If one tries to revisit the events, particularly with this trinity, it is, well … even Madame de Staël said that it was no easy task trying to write the story of Faust.

To return to the moment: After Heine left, Goethe sat alone in his living room without candlelight, and only stood up after a long while.

Heine sat in a carriage on his way to France. The fields outside were obscured by a dense fog. Heine was thinking about something that didn't seem worth the thoughts.

Halo

IN THE EAST and in the West, artistic representations of
deities, saints, or erudite monks invariably portray a halo
around or above the head. Eastern paintings and statuary
tend to present the frontal view of such images so that the
halo, you might say, is properly positioned. Such a ten-
dency at one time gained momentum and evolved into
such forms as the Buddhist dharma-wheel and deity images
of exceedingly extravagant designs. The western tradition,
on the other hand, was satisfied with simply positioning a
circle or an arc without any decorative intention, the effect
of which is quite clean and visually pleasant. Unfortunately,
however, when occidental paintings and statuary discarded
a frontal perspective and adopted a side profile—or par-
tial side profile—view, the halo needed to turn in propor-
tion to the angle of the view and thus it ended up looking
like an oval-shaped iron ring, or a bronze plate, precariously
suspended above the head, causing so much anxiety. How

could this possibly be the light of the divine! It appears absolutely ridiculous, so ridiculous that it is an eyesore.

In ancient times into the Middle Ages, perhaps image-making artists in the western world didn't understand the many dimensions in space or how light works by degrees, although they did know quite a bit about anatomy and perspective. Yet depicting this ray of light above the head contradicts rudimentary rules of physics. If the halo were accurately revealed in an image according to the laws of anatomy and perspective, it would appear completely out of place and visually offensive. What otherwise could be a fine work of art would be regrettably marred and fail because of a single detail. The evident irony is this: all halos, if placed above the heads of deities, saints, and erudite monks, are false and awkward additions—a serious visual examination informed by honesty and a knowledge of nature will be enough warning for artists to not be too willful. And yet, can this be blamed on artists alone?

That I've always been unable to convert myself into a follower of a western religion can perhaps be attributed to my discovery of this ludicrous flaw. Oh, Lord almighty! The flaw is so embarrassing that it further inspires the eloquence of atheists.

That I've always been unable to convert myself into a follower of an eastern religion can perhaps be attributed to my discovery of the excessive and baroque designs of the dharma-wheel and deity portraits. Oh, the designs are so refined, so extravagant, so blindingly bright, that one cannot have a single moment of internal tranquility.

So far I've only spoken of the "ridiculous." There are other things that border on the "painful."

The older generation of Chinese scholars all know something about the life of Master Hong Yi (the Buddhist name of Li Shutong). Li Shutong was well-educated in literature, music, and painting, and became a master of calligraphy. He was once also an excellent dramatic actor, and even gender-crossed the role of Madame Camille. Li traveled east to study in Japan, emerging as a scholar who defied a world of chaos with grace. He became a role model and star of his generation. But before he left China, he had apparently married. And so upon his return with a Japanese wife, his first wife caused an enormous uproar. It is said that Li wasn't able to resolve this peacefully and as a result lost all his worldly desires and became disillusioned with this physical, mundane world of ours. He then left for Lin Yin Temple in Hangzhou where he shaved his head and was initiated into the secluded life a monk. When his two wives rushed to the Flying Cliff, he had already chosen the practice of *zuo guan*—meditation in seclusion. *Zuo guan* is a ritual of voluntary imprisonment. The head bonze of a temple would personally seal the door of a room with some paper strips, symbolically turning the room into a secluded place, the paper strips not permitted to be removed until an agreed-upon date of release. Only meal boxes and water jars were passed in and out of the room through a small window. The two wives of the Li family knelt in front of the room and wailed, begging their husband to change his mind. For a whole day and a whole night there was absolute silence in the room, not a word issued forth in response to their wailing, revealing Li's undaunted determination. Admirable indeed is Hong Yi's firm resolution!

Uncle Zhao was a close friend of Master Hong Yi. It was the day I went to pay my respects to Zhao's mother at her birthday party that I saw a calligraphy scroll of the Vajracchedika Sutra copied out by Master Hong Yi as a special gift for Uncle Zhao's mother. The calligraphy was impressive, displaying perfect control—neither flashy nor mundane—and the use of ink was neither too watery nor too dry. There are so many calligraphic copies of Buddhist scriptures that are alike, but this scroll seemed to have risen from a unique hand—it was one thing to observe the solid foundational skills evident in the brushstrokes, and quite another thing to see its internal calmness bordering on the state of sainthood. I was in awe facing the art of a pure mind. I examined this copy of holy scripture very closely and felt a pleasure and admiration I couldn't express in words. I didn't dare continue looking at it.

On several occasions I had seen Master Hong Yi's calligraphy hanging on the walls of the wealthy. His brushstrokes always conveyed an extraordinary calm. Yet I also felt an aversion thinking that this monk had wasted his ink connecting with such people. Even if one adopted the view of the Mahayana, the Great Vehicle of Buddhism, that all living creatures deserve to be rescued and brought to transcendence, I would still say that Hong Yi also desired to please rich people. And it certainly didn't seem right if he was trying to collect alms. I was in a dilemma: it seemed more difficult to sympathize with the worldly intentions of a monk than that of a common man.

Uncle Zhao was a famous scholar, urbane and upright. A lay Buddhist himself, he was well versed in both Buddhism and Confucianism and had attained a high level of wisdom. I accompanied him one day on an excursion and we conversed over refreshing tea. He mentioned that shortly before Master Hong Yi passed away, he had gone hiking with him through the Yandang Mountains. Standing side by side with Hong Yi on top of a mountain, they both felt the high winds of the heavens and were silent. Their internal world was pure and expansive. However, as one's countenance always betrays signs of one's thoughts, Uncle Zhao noticed a subtle change in Hong Yi's eyes, and so he quietly asked, "I sense you have some thoughts?"

"I do."

"What do they concern?"

"Worldly matters ... family matters."

Uncle Zhao ended the story with a sigh: "If even Hong Yi who had attained such a high level of wisdom couldn't disconnect himself from worldly matters toward the end of his life, how could you or I, people who live mediocre lives?"

I wasn't quite twenty at the time, but the story touched me so deeply that I can distinctly recall it to this day. Uncle Zhao was always cautious about what he said and never gossiped about anyone. He told the story to me only because he was a close friend of my father's. I suspect he never repeated it to anyone else after sharing it with me that day. I cherish the story as much as I cherish the Buddha's sarira.

Uncle Zhao possessed sensitive instincts and was courageous in making his inquiry. Master Hong Yi was forthright and sincere in his response. If he had answered "I don't have any thoughts," or had tried to hide behind some vague metaphysical discourse, I would have been horrified, for such hypocrisy is vile. That Hong Yi gave a straightforward answer is remarkable and discloses the undying light of his internal world. It is a light more marvelous than any light added for decoration—that dull light resembling a circle or plate. I'm willing to forget my other impressions of Hong Yi, whether good or bad, but I will preserve those few words of truth he uttered not long before his death. Many a tightly shut door opens of its own accord without any wind; any heart that beats and flows with blood.

I didn't ask Uncle Zhao if he had seen a halo around Hong Yi's head when he gave his reply. I didn't ask because I knew that the halo must have been there. It isn't that Uncle Zhao and I have somewhat different views—we have entirely different views. But better to have this kind of generational gap than to not have it.

The above illustrates the "painful," painful but bright. There's another kind of halo, however, that borders on the cruel, that exists in the dim realm of suffering.

One evening, a few friends and I sat in a corner of a bar, talking and drinking.

George, a biophysics student, said, "The human body constantly emits a strange light. One with extraordinary physical capabilities emits a stronger light that sometimes appears as a luminous purplish-blue, particularly visible around the head."

Song Tian, who was obsessed with UFOs, responded, "Visitors from outer space wear a cosmic attire that includes a helmet which is actually a halo like those depicted in ancient statuary and cave paintings. This is evident in the art of Egypt, Mexico, and Russia. Ancient peoples abstracted the halo from their memories and legends."

Ouyang, a painter and sculptor, took his turn to speak: "If the head is supported by a circle, the circle can help the viewer focus on the person's face." He smiled and then confessed, "Once, a halo appeared around my head."

Everyone was perplexed except Ouyang who, smiling, kept his silence. Only after a long pause did he begin slowly:

"In the second half of the twentieth century, during a certain decade, certain events akin to religious persecution of heretics occurred in a certain country. I wasn't exactly a heretic, but certain details of a sculpture of mine were used against me. Before I realized what was happening, I was arrested and locked up. The cell I was put in wasn't more than twenty square meters—walls on three sides and one side iron bars—but it was crowded with fifty or so prisoners. During the day, we either sat or stood so that there was some room between us, but at night when everyone needed to sleep, you couldn't lie on your back but had to lie on your side with your legs stretched out so that your stomach touched the back of the person in front of you and your back stuck to the stomach of the one behind you. Summer nights the humidity was unbearable. Everyone sweated profusely....Well, this isn't what we were talking about, was it? So, going back to the halo...

"The days were very long; the young, the middle aged, and the old were all mixed together; only those with senior prison-status had the privilege of sitting against the walls, while newcomers stood in the middle of the room. When you have nothing to lean on to rest, your back hurts like hell and the passing of a day feels like a year. According to prison regulations, we were forbidden to reveal our names or to discuss the nature of our arrest. Thus we were also forbidden to ask about other people's names or arrests. I kept these rules in mind and wasn't going to divulge any information. Nor was I interested in talking to anyone. After two months, I was lucky enough to earn the privilege of sitting against the wall. The difference to my back was extraordinary. Indeed, sitting there was even enjoyable. I watched the other prisoners whispering to each other, killing time. So when the white-haired elderly man sitting next to me softly inquired for the third time, 'What are you here for, sir?' I replied in a low voice, 'Sculpting got me into trouble.' The old man was overjoyed at meeting a fellow artist, for he himself was a renowned art critic and painter. He leaned against my shoulders and whispered gently into my ear, 'Don't feel disheartened, don't ...' I felt that it was my turn to now ask, 'How do you know I'm dis-

heartened?'The old man mysteriously said, 'From your appearance, I know you are exhausted following the path of
art and that you are disdainful of immoral actions, so you
are thinking of quitting.' I felt he was quite perceptive, as
my thoughts then were to never touch plaster or clay ever
again if I got out of there. The old man continued, 'You see
the bunch of dry bones I am. Still, I will keep painting until my bones become ash. Even then my ashes can be used
for color pigments. You're half my age. Why should you be
discouraged!' I replied, 'Even if I paint and sculpt till I die,
is that meaningful?' 'True,' the old man said, 'but is there
anything else more meaningful than what you do?' That
seemed right to the point. I had been an artist for so many
years, why should I turn to anything else? Though I hadn't
tried to do much else, those other things seemed more
meaningless to me than sculpture. I couldn't help turning
to look at the old man. His hair was silver but his eyes spar-
kled. He smiled an enigmatic smile and asked, 'Have you
seen an image of Buddha?' 'Yes,' I said. 'And there is a circle surrounding the head?' 'Yes, the light of Buddha,' I replied. The old man sucked in a breath and said, 'Do you
know where that comes from?' 'It's just there,' I said. 'That
may not be true.... Look, see the wall across from us?' I
looked but didn't see. 'Look at the head positions of those
seated against the wall,' he said. Miraculously, I could suddenly make out a hazy circle behind the head of each prisoner. With so many heads repeatedly rubbing against the
chalky surface, sweat had tainted patches of the wall in circular shapes. Since everyone was of a different height, the

repeated rubbing produced circles of proportionate size to the heads before them. The circles were exactly like the dignified light of Buddha portrayed in ancient art. Not only that, each new prisoner had to have his head shaved. Our arms were bared as it was the peak of summer, and we sat with legs folded. Our posture, the hazy circles, the shaved heads formed eighteen arhat profiles, no more, no less. I almost burst out laughing—the subtle profundity had to be felt not just spoken. I was lifted up by the old man's humor, which is indispensable in coping with suffering, though his testimony far exceeded the force of humor.

"The old man was happy that I understood; his spirit was raised. Ever since then, we've been best friends despite our difference in age."

From the eyes of the few listeners present and the laughter, Ouyang received the appreciation he hoped for.

We raised our glasses. While we didn't quite know why we needed to empty the glasses, we emptied them anyway.

Tomorrow, I'll Stroll No More

I BUY CIGARETTES at the cross street and light one. Perpendicular to the street where I stand is a road lined with dwarf trees already filled with shiny new leaves. The taller trees on my street still display the grayness of bare branches. I imagine these must be budding too, but because of their height the branches aren't visibly green until their buds unfurl into leaves. I walk across the street and am soon back on the front steps of my apartment building where I suddenly realize how much I hate the stuffiness inside. The air outside is fresh. As air belongs to everybody it's also mine. I quicken my steps away and feel a sensation like swimming in the air, through waves of breeze. In this area of Jamaica, Queens, all the roads that diverge from Midland Parkway become a slope; the streets are bordered by wide or narrow lawns and by detached houses concealed behind tall trees; windows and doors of various styles are shut so tight that not a sound from within can be heard. The cleanness and quietness of the houses are impressive to me. Should some passerby say to me that none of them are inhabited, I won't be able to prove otherwise. At least right now, this moment in the afternoon. Only the glow of windows at night could indicate if one was occupied. Still, if a reclusive elderly lady dies in one of the houses, her lights would remain on for she wouldn't have been able to turn off the lights before she died. Her windows could continue to glow for weeks. It would then be the lights, not the dead lady, who suffer. It's fortunate that objects have no senses or the world would be infinitely more chaotic. It's fortunate that we live among objects with no senses so we can find places to hide, so we can easily move, rest, frown, smile at will, which is what we've been doing from one generation to the next into the present. Today I'm taking a stroll as I wasn't exactly taking one yesterday in the heavy rain. Through the hazy maze of Manhattan, I was sharing an umbrella with a friend. Either the two of us were too big or the umbrella was too small—we quickly got drenched save our hair. We entered the library to pay the fine I had received last month. Whoever first thought of imposing a library fine was indeed intelligent. Why don't we sit down and read, my friend suggested. I suspected that the soles of my shoes were cracked because my socks were soaked. You cannot read with feet in wet socks and shoes. So we walked back outside. New York in pouring rain gives one the illusion that there is no New York. When it pours in London, too, there is only rain and no London. Imagine two armies in ancient times engaged in battle on a plain, their flags fluttering and waving, soldiers on horseback falling to the earth when, all of a sudden, it starts to rain. The rain would become a primary force and the battle secondary. This was what the two of us talked and laughed about as if New York were nonexistent. Behind the iron-wrought fence of a bank I spied some yellowish white flowers that resembled a kind of autumn chrysanthemum I used to admire in China. I cried out: Look! Chrysanthemums are growing on trees and how awkward they appear in the pouring rain! My friend said: A tree full of dejected flowers ... it must be some kind of woody plant. Us humans are indeed wordy. We try to name anything we like or dislike. When we discover the name of something we feel contented and relaxed, but if we cannot name what we see or hear, we become slightly shy, vaguely apologetic, and mildly bashful. In this foreign land, I've felt dumb countless times not being able to name certain plants. Some purple flowers in bloom I think must be some type of lily magnolia blossom as they couldn't be those of the *yulan* or *mulan* magnolia, but who knows what Americans call them. The flower buds are smaller and thinner than the Chinese varieties of lily magnolia. I often don't have the confidence to identify even common plants and trees such as the maple, azalea, iris, and narcissus, if the variety looks slightly strange to me. One day I will return to China and will once again be able to call most of the plants by their Chinese names. I already feel happy knowing I still can. My own name isn't difficult to pronounce, but Westerners have to practice it, spell it out again and again, often smiling as they do so. Courtesy, culture, and the arts make people in this world slightly shy, vaguely apologetic and mildly bashful. In times of peace, people from different national and ethnic backgrounds can still communicate, coexist, cooperate.... When a war breaks out, we don't feel shy or apologetic or bashful toward each other, so of course war is terrible, so terrible indeed. Diametrically opposed to war is music. No matter how remote the country is that you travel to, when you hear music, particularly the music of your childhood, it's as if you're no longer lost, drifting on a boat during a stormy night, but suddenly floating into the harbor of your homeland, knowing that someone, regardless of wind or rain, is expecting you. I know a handyman, an elderly American man, who sometime works in the basement of my apartment building. He can really whistle. Many times I've heard him whistle and it's the essence of Father Haydn and Mozart the Son, without a hint of Uncle Sam. Once I responded with my own whistling. He stepped closer to listen, apparently surprised that the whistling of this Chinese man could evoke such a pure tune of the First Viennese School. In relation to music, another riddle demands explanation. When human beings cry, laugh, yawn, and sneeze, these actions are universally understood. So why are there so many complex, disparate language systems in this world? Animals don't have such complex language systems and so we've assumed they're dumb and inferior. Humans have created so many language schools, yet they walk in and out of them silent and sad. What then does life mean? Life means that you often don't know what to do.... I often lose my way, especially when I run an errand or try to make it to an appointment. If this happens late at night and I see a person standing in a parking lot, I'll quickly approach him. He says: I'll tell you how to get there but can you give me a cigarette? I'm happy to give him a cigarette, thinking that it's hard to find one's way and he'll need a cigarette to help him give clear directions. He inhales and inhales again before he points his finger and says: Two blocks from here. I feel very happy and even savor his humor. Suppose, though, I already know my destination is only two blocks away but see he badly needs a cigarette, and as I approach him he thinks I want to ask for directions but instead I greet him with a good evening, hand him a cigarette, light it for him, and walk away. That would be wonderful! But this doesn't really happen because you don't know if a stranger even smokes or, if he does, has run out of cigarettes. The feeling of swimming in fresh air that inspired you at the start of your stroll will eventually disappear. A breeze—a clear, passing breeze—brings a strong scent of flowers. I look around but don't see any flowers and cannot figure out where the aroma is coming from. Humans, not unlike canines, store memories of the past through scents, and a scent, at this moment, is what swiftly takes me back to those springs of my college years, to the narrow street in that colonized city in China, where the flower shops, record stores, and restaurants of the French concession scrolled on and on, where residents and businessmen were primarily Jewish, where there was an artificial Parisian mood, where White Russian drunkards and beggars loitered, where bookshops stayed silent while record stores roared, where the sweet smell of simmering tomato sauce drifted out of restaurants, where brewing coffee gave away half its essence to passersby for free, where the dense aroma from flower shops flooded the street. On clear, warm afternoons, with subtle smells swirling in the air, sunlight shone through tree leaves, dividing the street into shadowy, bright patterns. And if two ex-lovers met by chance on that street, the one who first noticed the other would walk head lowered. The college wasn't too far from the street. Rivaling students frequented the bookstores and bars in the vicinity. They secretly harbored their soaring ambitions, although after a few cups of cherry brandy, they'd feel so profoundly sad about their great futures that they wouldn't be in the mood to sympathize with the poor White Russian men and women in the streets, let alone consider that the same poverty might await them in their futures. Strong scents flowed in waves, but the sweetest and most potent emanated from carnations and *linglan*. American carnations only smell vaguely of grass; on the stone-paved narrow paths here in this neighborhood, *linglan* is often planted. When you bend your knees to get a good whiff of them, well, you smell nothing and feel like the mute or blind. *Linglan*, or hyacinth as it's called here, is of the lily family: narrow, long leaves sprout from the roots and grow in clumps; a single, central long stem produces flowers, each resembling a bell, its six petals in a racemed inflorescence of blue, purple, or pink. How can hyacinth so stately and aromatic appear so idiotic here? I suspect my judgment of flowers is wrong. After all, one's judgment of other people is often wrong, too. I must be wrong. If one day I return to China, I'll see the *linglan* hyacinths again; I'll gaze at them tenderly and obediently, bend my knees to sniff, and gaze again, remembering a flower in the United States that looks so much like them but has no aroma. So the breeze that just blew was a coincidence and is now gone forever. That was a three-year college, though I only attended for two-and-a-half years. Leaving the college meant leaving that street. We often leave without saying good-bye properly. Thirty years later colonization is now an outdated idea: the French, the Jews, and the White Russians are all gone; the street is gone; the college is gone. Once I asked a local about the college and she pointed to a huge gray warehouse used for cold storage and said that was where the college had been. How could it be? How could a street simply vanish? I explored five more streets and found no trace of what I could remember—nothing left resembled the past. I stood there foolishly looking for nothing. Now I must look quite foolish standing here waiting for another breeze to bring me the scent of flowers.... I start walking again. There are very few pedestrians. Those who appear walk very fast. My slow pace betrays me as a stroller. Taking a stroll is not a bad habit, but a man walking leisurely on a path in the spring, without a dog and near dusk, somehow seems embarrassingly out of place. This world where no one cares to watch or reproach you is still one in which you are watched and reproached. Those free souls in cities who escape to forests and ice-covered lands are perhaps trying to free themselves from the overwhelming feeling of being controlled. There used to be many hermits in ancient China, so many that people eventually classified them: the great hermits hid themselves in top administrative positions, the lesser ones concealed themselves in non-government jobs, and the still lesser ones in wilderness. This may sound fine and meaningful, though in practice, neither is a strict category. After all, those who tried to hide in all three situations sought the same thing. Feelings, freed of all external boundaries, are still confined within us—their sensitivity often causing bewilderment. I initially think the strong scent is wafting from the leaves above my head, but I soon realize it's freshly mowed grass. So many sliced grass-blades are indeed enough to evoke a cool and refreshing smell; but it's the green blood of brutally injured grass.... Evening descends and I near the end of my stroll. People like us are no longer capable of surviving outdoors day and night. We work at a table, sleep in a bed. To reproduce, to love or die, we need a house. These houses in Jamaica somehow resemble those in fairy tales, they exist somewhere between the legends of the aristocrats and fantasies of the commoners, narrating a story of the petty bourgeois, as if the aristocrats, in declining, lost their crown of glory, and the commoners, in climbing, lost their simplicity. Every house has this air. I remember those fairy-tale houses of my childhood, their colorful depictions in books. I remember making similar models—as a child in art class—with cardboard and glue. As

I observe each house one after another on my stroll, I see that a few of them intelligently apply the techniques of straight lines, oblique lines, and arches, but the surface textures and paint colors are wrong in most cases and will continue to be wrong, as if they only exist to display their mistakes to the world. One experiences pleasure when one sees houses constructed the right way. Yet, on second thought, one worries if the residents within might be stupid or mean, just as one worries if an intelligent and beautiful family lives in a poorly constructed house. Such formalist concerns don't apply to a minister walking out of a church or a clergyman standing on the steps of a monastery. Monuments are philistine, erected to illustrate the extremely poor memory of humans. Towers are best. Towers without hollow interiors are wonderful to gaze at from a distance. Other towers are hollow inside so that one can walk up the stairs to the top and enjoy a limitless expanse of scenery. It is quite appropriate that no one is permitted to live in a tower. Imagine if smoke from cooking poured out of a tower, or a clothesline was hung outside a tower window. This would cause such an uproar that the intended meaning of the tower would be forgotten. A well-designed tower embodies an architectural theme. When a tower is first completed, people surround it, crane their necks to look at it, they talk about it, a tide of voices rise and fall and then fade, while the original meaning of the tower also fades through the years so that if a bell hanging in the corner of the tower should fall, no one would bother to fix it. From the flowers of spring through the fruits of autumn, the tower stands just as a tower, seemingly in vain but in fact essential and inevitable. The phenomenon of building a group of towers in Southeast Asia is a misinterpretation of, and an insult to, the concept of a tower. Tower-ness is fated solitude that defies praise. The houses in Jamaica are not solitary. The space between each reflects human practicality, and contributes to the modesty and pride indispensable to the petty bourgeois: a cement swan, a freshly painted dwarf carrying a lantern, a sign announcing a certain doctoral degree, a garage added with a basketball rack—I have come to know these houses but their inhabitants I will never really know. The seasonal changes of scenery in Jamaica decide the routes of my strolls. On my return home, I make an unnecessary detour. It's unnecessary because when the stroll is no longer a stroll, not choosing a straight line between two points is considered a mistake. That objects can neither feel nor speak is fortunate—otherwise, I would be mocked by the houses and plants on my return. They would say, You could even lose your way when taking a stroll. I realize what life is. Life is constantly not knowing what to do. Therefore I let things happen to me—a breeze that brings a street filled with the scent of flowers, a tower whose meaning is obscured although it's still watched from a distance, a battlefield soaked in the rain while I talk loudly with a friend under a small umbrella. When something loses its first level of meaning, a second level of meaning emerges. The second level of meaning is often more accessible and more suitable for me: a baby stroller leaning against a tombstone, a three-page will found under a freshly baked loaf of bread. I stroll during a pleasant afternoon and lose my way in the second level of meaning. I have no other real pleasure. Often, just as I'm about to feel a small degree of pleasure, I feel a deep sadness. What is sadness? If I knew what sadness was, I would no longer feel sad. What then does life mean? Life means certain things are not yet done and must be done, and other things are done but not done well. Tomorrow, I'll stroll no more.

The Windsor Cemetery Diary

AT FIRST THE CEMETERY was foreign and nameless, but I've been taking leisurely walks through it once or twice a week for several years and its seasonal changes no longer astonish me. It didn't take me long to realize that this is a deserted place, a solitary enclave, as I never encountered anyone. As I stroll along the circular dirt footpath, I pass dark green trees and more dark green trees. Around the outer edge of the path are fourteen tombstones, and inside the circle is a large lawn of fine grass where two species of towering trees make a shady, quiet wood. At the center of this enclosure there is a large, dark rock that leans toward the west, its elephantine back curving above the tall grass. It's so tempting to rest upon it, not because I'm fatigued but because it's the perfect spot to watch the intertwined branches above, a sky full of bright green leaves, quivering and rustling.

The previous summer was marked by strong winds

and unusually severe rainstorms. Some trees in the cemetery cracked—one that fell in the northwest corner was later sawn into segments and left exposed; in the sunlight I could see the faint yellowish flesh of the tree's stump and could count a hundred of its rings; a hollowed section was filled with insects, and it seemed the tree hadn't injured any of the surrounding trees when it fell. In the summer the northwest corner is unusually bright in contrast to the deep shade that covers the rest of the cemetery; I imagined the fallen tree once thick with leaves, and it wasn't until autumn, late autumn, that my sense of loss became less pronounced when all the logs of the tree had been removed, and by next summer one could not even tell that there had been any loss in the cemetery unless one remembered the fallen tree.

(I should include these thoughts in my letter to Sandra.)

The dark rock, enormous in girth, occupies a spot from which an orchestral conductor might stand, though this particular conductor idly sits there smoking, listening to the counterpoint of leaves in the cemetery, immersing himself in the joys and the glories of the music that pay homage to him while he imagines his own body is a thin paper boat and the sounds of the leaves rippling water on which the boat freely floats....

Those myriad sounds tickle the fine hairs in the ears, and the breeze feels cool and moist on the hair and skin, but this is not all the idle body feels, for it refuses to be ignored and abandoned and stretches because a healthy body stiffens if it remains on that dark rock too long, it stretches because a body requires stretching and adjusting before it can slowly restore itself.

The body wants to leave the dark rock but doesn't know where to go—it only knows that it cannot remain in the same position too long, and in fact the body is sensitive to the slightest hint of death and remaining too long in the same position means bordering on death, which is why the adjustment of limbs proves to the body its existence, renews its suspicion of death-like conditions. Only illness or sleep returns some quiet to the body as the body then knows it cannot continue to exist unless illness is cured and sleep satisfied; yet the body cannot remain still after it has recovered or awakened, for whenever there is a long period of stillness, the body receives warning signals from sore bones or itchy skin, and if such signals are ignored more deceptive tricks follow: the body feigns obedience and calmness, discontent rises from within, senses numb and the myriad sounds no longer evoke joy and splendor, and then what use is it to remain on the dark rock?

Why is taking a stroll so suitable for meditation? As the body follows the course of the body and the soul follows the course of the soul, the soul can assign a task to the body, leaving the body no extra energy to meddle with the soul, and the body also becomes content, aimless and wandering, not feeling its labors, cheerfully carrying the soul while moving of its own accord. Indeed, most types of meditation are conspiracies devised to subdue the body, or cause its illusory elimination.

(The above should be sent to Sandra. No, I don't think she'd complain that I'm making my letter longer than usual.)

This is not a public burial ground for everyone—it is a portion of the Church's property. All the deceased are Christians who were once ministers. Beyond the trees is the cement plaza that is filled with parked vehicles on Sunday mornings. These buildings, rough stone façades of yellowish gray, make up a monastery built in a simple yet grand style rare even in North America. The empty plaza is like an expanse of water. Occasionally I can glimpse a couple of human figures who appear to be neither *monachus* nor *nonna*. If they are not clergymen living in this monastery, they must belong to another order. There are those who have chosen to abandon worldly affairs and live a disciplined religious life, and others who share the same tenets and become members of the same parish, dedicating their lives to the sharing of the gospel, to building and running schools, to offering blessings. It is historically inaccurate to say that such ways of life have nearly died out after four hundred years. Monastic orders originated in the fifth and sixth centuries. When the Crusaders reeled back for the seventh time, it was those in black robes who nursed European culture to keep it from dying at a desolate station on the pilgrimage to Heaven.

I'm certainly interested in finding out if the cemetery

has a specific name, but I also wonder if my long familiarity with it allows me to name it myself, as it isn't uncommon for us to call out to strangers in the darkness, either in intimate tones or through grinding teeth, which is to say, we give them names when the ordinary becomes extraordinary.

The designs of the tombs vary. Buried underneath could be ashes, not bodies. On top of the soil that covers the ashes is a platform more than a meter high built of rows of rectangular coal-black stones. The headstone sits on the platform. In the lower right hand corner of the headstone is a small, rectangular bronze plate bearing the name of the deceased, the date of birth, and the date of death; in the center is a porcelain square with the image of a human body in relief. Although the arbors of summer green initially led me to this cemetery, what brings me back for frequent visits are fourteen different porcelain reliefs. Christ is embodied in these different selves so that his repetitions are never tiring to the eye. On a blank background, these porcelain squares depict his figure on the cross: his emaciated, tall, ascetic body; his robe with folds, glazed in light shades of turquoise and crimson—these details conveying the spiritual. The clay is rough and grainy, and of similar transparency to the sad and morbid yellow in the porcelain square. There is a sense of remote time and space, the portrayal of the human figure in a Byzantine style that invites a prolonged gaze. By the time of the Byzantines, great artists seemed to have gone to sleep, leaving all the work to craftsmen. Art became both mellow and crude. If the craftsmen were not sincere, the style would not have been so crude, though as it is crude, what affects us the most is its sincerity.

(Sandra likes my wordiness. I might as well send her these words. She believes her loneliness in Geneva is real, implying that my loneliness here is false. I once told her that if she could distinguish real loneliness from false loneliness, maybe she really wasn't lonely.)

The plate on the fifth tombstone is missing, revealing a dark hazel spot in the lower right-hand corner.

The other thirteen tombstones remain intact. But one of them bears no name of the deceased, making one wonder *who* might be buried underneath.

Once again my eyes scan the grass, half hoping to find the missing plate somewhere near the platform.

On the platform is a penny. A coin may be dropped accidentally on the footpath or in the grass, but how could it end up on the platform so high above the ground?

I pick up the coin, and for some reason when I place it back down I feel a sense of emptiness and bewilderment. I end my walk disappointed—an incomprehensible occurrence is frustrating.

(I include these thoughts in my diary to show that there is nothing to be recorded.)

Edward VIII and Wallis Simpson, famous lovers of the twentieth century, have now become part of the past. Newspapers around the world mourned her death as if they were holding a retrospective exhibition for an artist. Photos of the younger Wallis glamorized the newspapers for several days.

Because the exhibition looks retrospectively at the love between the Duke and the Duchess of Windsor, worldly men and women seize the occasion to recall their own experiences of falling in and out of love.

This has clearly been a most vulgar century—both brutal and overly sentimental. No wonder when people today suddenly find themselves remembering the Duke and Duchess of Windsor, what seems to be a mildly classical fragrance greatly confuses them, so much so that they feel, all too sadly, that time is being pulled backward. Some wonder aloud: Is love real and really possible?

Who knows in what era someone first thought, Life is like a dream. Before then, who had heard such a figure of speech? Life is like a dream: those who heard it must have felt the lightning bolt of a revelation, and spread the sentiment widely until everyone was saying it. From this we can deduce another story of remote antiquity. Someone— a man or woman, we cannot know—was the first ever to say to the person closest to his or her heart, "I love you." Following the same logic, there must have been someone who first created the word "love" and placed an "I" before it and a "you" after it. Those who heard the sound of "I love you" and who saw those words for the first time must have felt the most intense ecstasy, for who could've thought that heartfelt passions could be translated into the sounds of words? Afterward, for generations of men and women born into this world, the word "love" became so overused in speeches and writing that it became stale, awkward, and clumsy. This is why when the lovers of Windsor announced their love with such clear voices and wrote about it in such a neat hand, others once again felt that life is life and dream is dream, and once again thought: life is like a dream. In fact, at that moment, these people exist in life and not in dream.

At Cartier's in Paris, at different times Edward VIII purchased for Wallis a whole range of jewelry, totaling eighty-seven items.

From Van Cleef and Arpels, he purchased twenty-three items, including a necklace of rubies set around diamonds, bearing this inscription: My Wallis. David.

A sapphire watch encased in diamonds, also purchased from Van Cleef and Arpels, is inscribed: For our engagement: 18V-37.

From Cartier's, a ruby bracelet with diamonds for their first wedding anniversary, June 3rd.

An evening handbag decorated with pearls and diamonds.

Belts and mirrors encased in precious stones.

Leopard-shaped and tiger-shaped bracelets and hair clips set with Cartier's famous cat's-eye cabochons.

A red crane pin decorated with rubies, sapphires, jade, and diamonds.

A total of two hundred and sixteen items. As if words were not enough, the Duke of Windsor used jewelry to enhance his expression of love to Wallis, the woman for whom he abdicated his English throne. She was, perhaps, innocent, or at least despondent, her whole life; the royal family and upper class society secretly watched her as if she were a bad omen. It's said that before her death, for eight years she had secluded herself upstairs in her home at Boulogne, France, and for seven years had been unable to speak. Those two hundred and sixteen objects of love's promises have since been deposited in a bank; they could remain frozen there forever, no longer shimmering with the crystal in the candlelight.

The deepening of autumn doesn't mean bleakness in the cemetery. Trees are denuded of leaves and their fine twigs reflect the azure of the sky. Their splendor delights the eye in the season of their nakedness. Summer is the season of naked humans, as winter is the season of naked trees.

My speculation that the cemetery is deserted has been proven wrong. It's no longer my own solitary enclave. The coin placed on the platform of the fifth tombstone has been flipped over. I remember when I first picked it up and put it down, Lincoln's portrait faced up. Now it shows his Memorial.

Someone else has seen this penny, picked it up, and replaced it.

I flip the coin back to the side of Lincoln's portrait.

Several days later I return to the cemetery to find the Memorial facing dim twilight.

A message. Between the portrait, which is my side, and the Memorial, which is the Other's, there is a message. The heads and tails of the message are linked. Other than that, there is neither beauty nor ugliness, wisdom nor folly, strength nor weakness. Anyone can pick up the coin between the thumb and index finger and turn it over.

No wind, or rain, or snow can make the flat coin flip; birds will not peck it; squirrels only follow their sense of smell to look for food—whatever turns the coin from heads to tails is a human force.

I, the head; the Other, the tail; after turning the coin several times, the message deepens:

I exist.

I do not forget.

I am willing to continue.

As the heads-to-tails turning increases, the message acquires a new value:

I am the reason that the Other still exists.

How can I forget.

I can no longer discontinue this continuity.

At first, this is but a simple hand gesture using two fingers—the initial message is as natural as heads or tails—but as I and the Other, each representing a side, keep turning the coin, we create with our own hands a fated cycle that we fall into.

If I no longer visit the cemetery, or if I visit the cemetery without going near the fifth tombstone, or if I walk past the tombstone without turning over the coin—each of these three possibilities is immoral, almost sinful.

Execution grounds, casinos, battlegrounds are all places where brutality is exercised. Sotheby's is also such a place.

April 1987: Sotheby's in Geneva plans to sell the two hundred and sixteen promises of love the Duke of Windsor gave to the Duchess.

The Duchess has donated the majority of her property to the Pasteur Center, a medical research institution that cannot think of a more caring and appropriate way to handle these gifts of love than to submit them to Sotheby's who have them locked in a Geneva bank.

The voice of Sotheby's says: We have invited jewelry experts in Geneva to appraise this collection; it is only reasonable that we hold the auction for these items.

Does love need appraisal? When the jewelry experts appraise the love between the Duke and the Duchess, what should be priceless will be given a price.

April: a warm season suitable for growth. Switzerland: a fortunate country. Geneva: a city of clear lakes. Sotheby's: a place for exercising brutality.

The necklace of rubies and diamonds is insured by the bank for 600,000 pounds sterling. Experts, however, estimate its actual value at 500,000 pounds. An American film actress is the first to make an offer; a member of the Dubai royal family counters with a price of 550,000 pounds; a German steel tycoon bids 600,000 pounds, an amount that equals the insurance cost; the king of Greek shipping adds 20,000 to this amount. Then comes Mrs. X, widow of the platinum king, who had a close relationship with the Duchess of Windsor. She once saw Wallis wearing the ruby necklace at an evening party and was deeply impressed.

It is now February. Two more months remain. Sotheby's

has announced that the auction will take place under the most confidential conditions. Not even the list of guests will be made public.

Nearing the fifth tombstone....

Ordinarily a coin would just pass between my fingers without my careful examination, but now I read, on the obverse side just above the Lincoln Memorial, that line in Latin—*e pluribus unum*—which figuratively eulogizes this country. The eulogy, however, certainly doesn't limit the possibilities of what this can suggest.

Turning over the coin sends messages; not turning it over also sends messages, such as:

I am dead.

I have completely forgotten you.

I do not come anymore.

Apart from death, which is ordained by Heaven, the other two messages might be saying to the Other: I am frivolous and fickle. A judgment is then implied: the Other is a romantic fool, since only a fool will communicate for so long with someone frivolous and fickle.

It is also possible that the Other has fallen into the fated cycle and cannot break free from it. Or the Other is already tired of sneaking into the woods, morning and evening, just to turn the coin over. This possibility is my sorrow.

I'm afraid of the intrusion of a third person who might see the coin, pick it up, and throw it away. If this happens, there will be confusion and the messages will change:

Stop.

This is absurd.

Eliminate the absurdity.

If the coin is not there, the intrusion of a third person should be the first explanation. Then another similar coin should be placed there, with the portrait turned up.

I'm also convinced that if my Other finds the coin missing, my Other will, upon reflection, put another coin in the same place, with the Memorial turned up.

If so, is the essence of the situation not dissimilar to vows of love?

If the flipping of the coin is the work of either a divine will or a demonic will, it can be ignored—whatever tricks God or the devil plays on someone, this person can still be tenacious enough to deal with them. What is in question, however, is the human will. The gender, age, appearance, and personality of the Other are unknown. The more time that passes, the less I'm interested in knowing the personality, appearance, age, and gender of the Other. What I have in mind is a purely human thought. Is it not like the line in Latin: *e pluribus unum*?

(In her letter, Sandra says that her daughter has been admitted to a school nearby so that she can at last devote herself to her work as a journalist. As if I were one of her regular sources, she asks without explanation:

Are you coming in April? I mean, of course, the end of March. I'll be glad to take you to see those items the Duchess of Windsor has left behind. The most touching piece is, undoubtedly, the ruby necklace. Wallis Simpson was wearing it when I first met her at

Mrs. X's salon. She was forty then, pretty as a clear spring in the forest, a beauty unmatched by anyone of her generation. She belongs to the last century. Or, rather, hers is a nineteenth-century personality adrift in the twentieth.

I hope you can come. Of course you will have to resist the temptation of going to Sotheby's. If you end up deciding not to come, I wouldn't miss the six days of the exhibition, from March 17th to the 22nd, when it will be in New York. If you see it, at least you will have something to talk about later.

I imagine you must regret that the Duchess's personal things will soon be scattered. Being scattered means they will be lost, but I won't be able to persuade Mrs. X to purchase the whole lot. Oh, those wretched buyers! As for the ruby necklace, I have already lobbied the queen of platinum and made her furious enough to pledge that she will get it no matter what. How happy you would make me if you could come and see for yourself to whom the necklace will finally belong.

You know Wallis always lived in the shadows. Of course this means she also lived in David's love. When the Duke died, she turned gray. He and she had no cause; they only had their love. Just as you once mocked, love was their cause. Well, what of those who take such love as their cause?)

(My letter in reply: *I cannot come to Switzerland at the end of March. I'm not even sure if I can make the trip in April or May.*

I will come though. When I come I will tell you what has been happening here.

Please don't ask, and especially don't try to do your detective work over the phone. I cannot make myself clear. I know I can

count on your understanding. And please forgive me for not writ-
ing you for so long. I've stopped writing in my diary.

When I come to Geneva, I will bring something for you to
compare with the ruby necklace. I wouldn't speculate though—
you won't be able to guess what it is. It's neither good nor bad.
At any rate, I'll stop mocking those who take love as their cause,
but I will not stop mocking those journalists who uphold the news
about love as their cause. You're an exception because you know
you always are to me.

When the ruby necklace is on display at Sotheby's in New
York, I will pay homage to it as you asked me to—it will still be
a legendary and therefore sacred object. After that, after April, it
will become a vulgar piece of commodity. Yes, I am slightly dejected.
The world is so large, yet there is no hiding place for a woman's
jewelry. Why must they be dismembered like a corpse and scattered
about? It is indeed a sentimental education. I remember the auc-
tioning of Madame Arnoux's belongings, which happened when
she was still alive. That was cruelty, pure cruelty. Incidentally, lit-
erature is … it will succeed when you exquisitely fail at writing.)

I visit the cemetery every Friday now. One afternoon, I
found the coin had been turned over again. There was no
mistake about it. Ecstasy stung me like needles.

A few heavy snowfalls have piled up snow, particularly in
the north-west corner of the cemetery. I have now learned
to see a difference between the naked trees: some can hold
snow on their branches, others cannot. After a heavy snowfall, for instance, the arbor trees of varying heights still show
their branches, clean and bare.

When the coin is covered by the snow, I have an ominous feeling that the fated cycle has come to an end. I reach out my palm to tenderly brush the snow aside like someone looking for treasure, or a dead body.

February 6th. I've spent an entire day in Manhattan handling my worldly affairs. Not until I'm finished do I realize the depth of the snow and the depth of the night. Traffic is difficult. When I drive up to the church, the gate at the entrance is lowered, prohibiting one from parking. The silver-colored plaza is wide and spacious. In one of the monastery's upstairs windows, a light, seen through the snowflakes, glows a soft orange color. More than a month has passed since Christmas.

Falling snow on a windless day has a moist warmth. Under my steps, fresh white snow crackles, and I feel a strange mixture of guilt and gratitude. The silence on this snowy night is innocent the way the snow of a temperate zone has a childishness that won't last.

A thick layer of snow covers the platform of the tomb. My hand reaches into the surface beneath the snow. I pull out the coin. By the flame of my lighter, I see it clearly. I turn it over, push it into the snow, making sure it's flat on the stone.

The cemetery is enveloped in white, whirling snowflakes and seems quite foreign, recalling the snowy wilderness of my now distant childhood.

I light a cigarette. I already know and see that I'm known and seen.

(12:00 a.m., midnight. When we leave the cemetery together it is 3:30 in the morning. *E pluribus unum*. Snow
keeps falling.)

Translator's Afterword

More than twenty books by Mu Xin—an internationally renowned writer and painter—have been published in Taiwan and mainland China. The thirteen pieces of *An Empty Room*—his first collection of stories to appear in English—were specifically chosen by the author from three of his books: 《散文一集》(*Collected Sanwen: Volume 1*; 1986), 《温莎墓园》(*Windsor Cemetery*; 1988), and 《巴珑》(*Barron*; 1998).

Each story not only stands on its own as an individual work of fiction, but the collection as a whole can be read as a short story cycle, or a linked bildungsroman, written in varying first-person personae, each "I" embodying a different race, gender, history. This paradoxical coexistence of fragmentation and cohesiveness in one book is of course not an uncommon practice in modern literature, though it is essentially informed by Mu Xin's own aesthetic principle, namely: the self, the artistically transformed and transforming self, must live through others so that others can live through him. The other referring not only to another person but also to an other time-space, an other reality, an other experience. Mu Xin's style, which is influenced by both Chinese and world literature, and is simultaneously poetry, essay, and fiction, brings to light this relational other. It evokes the spirit of innovation in contemporary world literature and connects Mu Xin to the Chinese *sanwen*, a genre that freely crosses the boundaries of poetry, meditative essay, and fiction. Indeed, some of his texts were written in both prose and verse forms. In the Chinese tradition, Mu Xin admires the work of the eight great *sanwen* authors of the Tang and Song dynasties: Han Yu, Liu Zongyuan, Ouyang Xiu, Su Xun, Su Shi, Su Che, Wang Anshi, Zeng Gong. He also includes Nietzsche, Emerson, Rousseau, and Montaigne as some of his favorite authors that exemplify the *sanwen* spirit. In the best sense of the word, Mu Xin himself is a *sanwen* writer.

Mu Xin was born in 1927 in Wuzhen, Zhejiang Province. In his early years, he was exposed, through voluminous reading, to both the Chinese classical literati tradition and to Western artistic and cultural traditions. Part of this education was completed in the private library of Mao Dun, who was Mu Xin's distant uncle and a major figure in modern Chinese literature. From 1949 till 1982, Mu Xin lived in China, and as an artist survived some terrifying experiences, including an eighteenth-month imprisonment in an abandoned air-raid shelter. Bizarre as it may sound to us today, Mu Xin's case was commonplace in that time period. A person could be imprisoned without trial or sentencing and even without a legal court if he or she belonged to the "wrong" socal group (e.g., intellectuals) or showed "decadent" tendencies in thinking. Few works of Mu Xin's literary and artistic creativity from that period have survived. From 1982 till 2006, Mu Xin lived in the United States. This was a period of prolific and profound artistic and literary creativity in his life. I met Mu Xin in New York in the late 1980s when his literary works began to arouse great interest among diasporic Chinese intellectuals. In the following decades, his writing and paintings won great admiration around the world and established him as a revered artist–intellectual. During those years, I twice interviewed him on his life and art and subsequently published those interviews. In 2006, the year when he returned to China to live in his hometown, his works, previously unpublished and largely unknown in mainland China, were re-issued and became such an event that the publishing world in China called 2006 "the Year of Mu Xin."

I feel privileged that I've been able to work closely with Mu Xin to complete this translation. For the past decade or so I have continuously consulted him on issues relating to this book and have received direct advice from him about what details should be changed and what should not. Decisions in translation often concern details that initially seem trivial but are ultimately significant. In consultation with

Mu Xin, for example, I decided to use "Fong Fong," in the story "Fong Fong No. 4," as the English transliteration instead of using the strictly Chinese *pinyin* rendition of "Fang Fang," as the latter might cause confusing connotations in English. During the various stages of working on this collection, many other such choices were made, not to deviate from the original, but to try to capture the spirit of Mu Xin's stylized, elegant Chinese.

Over the years, Arthur F. Kinney, Donald Junkins, John Parker, Vilma Potter, Susan Harris, Ruben Quintero, Roberto Cantu, Timothy Steele, Chen Danqing, and Hugo Liu read parts of the manuscript in English and generously offered suggestions and m. I am grateful to the literary agent Joanne Wang for making the publication of this book possible. Last but not least, Jeffrey Yang from New Directions gave the entire collection a patient and thorough editing that graces my translation. I wish to acknowledge my heartfelt thanks to all of them.

TOMING JUN LIU
january 1, 2011

MU XIN, born in 1927 in the south of China, is the author of twenty collections of stories, poetry, and essays. He is also an internationally renowned painter. During the Cultural Revolution much of his work—manuscripts and paintings—was destroyed. He moved to the United States in 1982, living in Queens, New York, until 2006. He now lives in his hometown, Wuzhen, in Zhejiang Province. The thirteen stories in this collection were composed while Mu Xin lived in New York.

TOMING JUN LIU grew up in China and received his education in China, Britain, and the United States. He was a translator at the United Nations Secretariat in the early 1980s. He is now Professor of English at California State University, Los Angeles, and holds an endowed professorship at Hangzhou Normal University, China.